Repair Your Own Credit

3rd Edition

By

Bob Hammond

REPAIR YOUR OWN CREDIT

Cover design by Lu Rossman

Edited and typeset by Jodi Brandon

Printed in the U.S.A. by Book-mart Press

To order this title, please call toll-free 1-800-CAREER-1 (NJ and Canada: 201-848-0310) to order using VISA or Master Card, or for further information on books from Career Press.

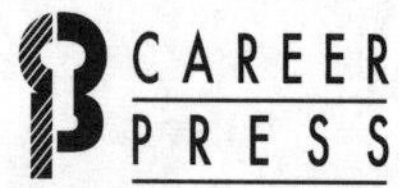

The Career Press, Inc., 3 Tice Road, PO Box 687,
Franklin Lakes, NJ 07417
www.careerpress.com

Library of Congress Cataloging-in-Publication Data

Hammond, Bob.
Repair your own credit / by Bob Hammond. — 3rd ed.
p. cm.
Includes index.
ISBN 1-56414-517-4 (paper)
1. Consumer credit—United States. 2. Credit ratings—United States. I. Title.

HG3756.U54 H367 2001
332.7'43—dc21

00-066714

Acknowledgments

There are many people who helped make this book a reality. They include Ron Fry, Jodi Brandon, Stacey Farkas, Jackie Michaels, Jennifer Seaman, and Mike Lewis at Career Press. Also, thanks to Anne Robinson, Betsy Sheldon, and Ellen Scher, who assisted with revisions for previous editions.

The original edition of this book would not have been possible without the support and assistance of the following people: Peder Lund, Jon Ford, Karen Pochert, Fran Milner, Janice Vierke, and Tina Mills at Paladin Press; Lona Luckett at the Better Business Bureau; Holly Novac at TRW (now Experian); Russell Deitch at the Federal Trade Commission; Gayle Weller and Susan Henrichsen with the California Attorney General's Office; Nancy Cox with the Riverside County District Attorney's Office; Elliot Blair Smith at the Orange County Register; Laurin Jackson at Secretarial Solutions; Lenny Robin of Fresh Start Financial Service; Dianne Huppman, Executive Director of Consumer Credit Counseling Service of the Inland Empire; Merrill Chandler of the North American Consumer Alliance; and Michael Jay, Michael Hsu, Ken Yarbrough, Greg Sullivan, Stacey Aldstadt, Carmen Vargas, June Lamond, Michael Givel, Jayson Orvis, Troy Smith, Mike Foccio, Ron Vervick, Ronda Roberts, Michael Hunter Schwartz, Joel Goodman, Brent Romney, Winfield Payne, Donna Jones, Ethan Ellenberg, and Kathy McSkimming. To these people, and to everyone else who made a contribution to this book—thank you.

Contents

Preface

Karen Johnson had recently returned from college in Europe and had not yet established credit in the United States. She picked out a small used car with a sticker price of $12,600 at Sam's Auto Mart. She filled out a credit application, and the salesman left to process it. When the salesman returned, he told Karen, "I'm sorry, but you don't have enough credit to qualify for the loan." Karen went to four other car dealers and got the same reaction. Slick Willie, the salesperson at Too Good Auto Sales, also told Karen that her credit history was insufficient, but he added that he could help her establish new credit. Karen, frustrated and in desperate need of a car, decided to go along with Slick Willie's plan.

Slick told Karen that he had a friend who, for $900, could get her a good credit rating. Slick also promised to reduce the sticker price of the car by that amount. Slick called his friend Felix Fixer and arranged a meeting for Karen and Felix.

Karen went to Felix's office and wrote him a check for $900. Felix went right to work. He called Blue Sky Bank, a subscriber to a major credit bureau. Felix convinced the bank clerk that he was an employee of a credit bureau and that, because of computer problems, he needed to get the bank's credit bureau access code. The clerk responded with the three-digit code.

Next, Felix searched the phone book for other people named Karen Johnson. He used the access code that he obtained from Blue Sky Bank to get credit information from the credit bureau on all of the Karen Johnsons listed in the phone book. When he found a credit report for a Karen Johnson that contained only positive information, he stopped looking. He copied down the account information, and then contacted Karen at home and asked her to stop by his office.

When she arrived, Felix gave her the credit information he had obtained and instructed her to use all of the information when filling out an application. He also instructed her to use a mail-drop address that he could control as her current address and to use the "victim's" Social Security number. Karen was now free to apply for credit anywhere.

Karen went back to Too Good Auto Sales and reapplied, using the new information. She got the car, Slick and Felix split the $900, and Slick Willie got the commission.

❑ ❑ ❑

This is just one example of the multitude of credit repair scams that have sprung up around the credit reporting industry, capitalizing on the credit problems of millions of American consumers and exploiting the weaknesses in the credit reporting industry. There are many more.

The flaws in the credit reporting system and the abuses that have occurred in the industry have caused financial injury to a significant number of consumers. However, these flaws and abuses spawned another whole industry (credit repair) that, although well-intentioned originally, has become riddled with corruption.

Consumers should be wary of credit bureaus and credit repair services alike. The fact is that consumers who wish to have false or inaccurate information removed from their credit reports have little need for credit clinics. Under the rules outlined in the Fair Credit Reporting Act, they can do it themselves easily and inexpensively.

Repair Your Own Credit was written for those consumers who have had credit problems and are considering the services of a credit repair company. It is meant to warn consumers of the dangers and pitfalls of credit repair and to empower people to help themselves. The book is a result of many years of research into the subject of consumer credit, including my own personal experiences as a credit consultant and consumer activist. It is based on firsthand accounts of some of the major players in the credit game.

Repair Your Own Credit takes a revealing, if not shocking, look at the scams and scoundrels that gave the credit repair business such a bad reputation and tells how they ended up. Many of my former associates have cautioned that I may be sacrificing my own livelihood and perhaps even my own freedom and safety by publicizing this book, and perhaps that is so. But to paraphrase Benjamin Franklin, "Those who would give up essential publicity to purchase a little security deserve neither."

Chapter 1

The Credit Game

For many years, I researched various strategies for attaining the personal and financial freedom that comes with debt-free wealth. I spent thousands of dollars on books, tapes, newsletters, and home-study courses. I attended seminars and consulted with self-proclaimed experts on real estate, creative financing, positive thinking, multilevel marketing, mail-order publishing, and other plans. Some were very valuable and informative; others were total rip-offs. I also came across several underground books that claimed to reveal inside secrets and strategies for beating the system. Some of these books contained very interesting and useful information. Others turned out to be not only completely illegal, but frightening as well.

I finally began to get discouraged. None of these plans lived up to their promises. The only people who seemed to be getting rich were the promoters themselves. I was tired of being ripped off. I still couldn't help thinking, however, that there must be a way for someone like myself, with an average education and abilities, to get ahead in the world.

One day I attended a seminar in Riverside, Calif., led by an authority on consumer credit. The seminar also featured a former credit bureau executive turned consumer advocate. I listened intently as they took turns explaining credit bureau operations, consumer rights under the Fair Credit Reporting Act (FCRA), how to have negative information removed from credit files, and the secrets of establishing a new credit identity. The final hour of the seminar was devoted to instructions on setting up a profitable credit consulting firm. I was intrigued by the possibilities. Somehow, this seminar seemed a little different than the others. Little did I know that it was about to become a major turning point in my life. I left the seminar with an entirely new understanding of the phrase "knowledge is power."

Eagerly, I began the process of clearing up the wreckage of my past and getting my own house in order. My credit had been devastated by bankruptcy, divorce, and many years of reckless living. I was amazed to discover that, by applying what I had learned at the seminar, in a matter of weeks, companies that had rejected me previously were suddenly begging me to take their credit cards.

For several years I worked as a credit consultant with my own company. By working with others, I discovered that most people had information in their credit files that was obsolete, inaccurate, or misleading. In many cases, the information belonged to someone else with a similar name. I discovered that people were being discriminated against and turned down for credit, insurance, jobs, and even places to live because of a clerical error.

During this time I was involved in a lawsuit against TRW Information Services (now called Experian), one of the largest and most powerful of the consumer credit reporting services or credit bureaus. That prompted me to do some additional research into the way credit bureaus violated the rights of citizens.

The culmination of this research was the publication of *How to Beat the Credit Bureaus: The Insider's Guide to Consumer Credit.* This book shows how credit bureaus violate the Fair Credit Reporting Act, and it presents case studies of people who have taken legal action against the bureaus on grounds of defamation, invasion of privacy, and negligence.

Consequently, hundreds of lawsuits were filed against the major credit bureaus throughout the country. TRW was among them, with the Federal Trade Commission (FTC) and 19 states filing lawsuits against it. The credit bureaus were forced to make it easier for consumers to obtain information regarding their files and also to dispute erroneous information. TRW and Equifax awarded thousands of dollars in damages to consumers and agreed to major concessions and policy changes.

Meanwhile, with 70 percent of American consumers as potential clients, the credit repair industry developed quickly to meet the needs of the millions of individuals with poor credit ratings. Along the way, a parade of con artists and self-proclaimed credit gurus took advantage of an opportunity, leaving behind a wake of bare-pocketed consumers. In recent years, American consumers have lost more than $50 million collectively by hiring fly-by-night operators to "fix" their credit reports—with little or no results. Thousands of consumers have complained of being ripped off by unscrupulous promoters of credit repair scams. In an attempt to put a stop to these companies and their deceptive practices, new legislation has been passed.

The following pages provide a shocking inside look at the scams used by credit clinics to bilk millions of dollars from gullible consumers on a daily basis. They also explain how you can work to repair your own credit, for little or no money.

[illegible] standards [illegible] were [illegible] with the Federal Trade Commission (FTC) and [illegible] complaints [illegible] consumers [illegible] and [illegible] information [illegible] and [illegible] to [illegible] changes.

[illegible] credit [illegible] a potential [illegible] industry [illegible] to meet the needs of [illegible] millions of individuals [illegible] credit [illegible]. Along the way, a [illegible] of con artists and self-proclaimed credit [illegible] took advantage of an [illegible] market, leaving behind a wake of [illegible] consumers. [illegible] recent years, [illegible] consumers [illegible] that [illegible] their credit [illegible] results. Thousands of consumers have complained of being ripped off by [illegible] companies [illegible] deceptive practices [illegible] legislation has been passed.

The following pages provide [illegible] look at the [illegible] used by credit [illegible] consumers [illegible]. They also explain how you can [illegible] your own credit [illegible].

Chapter 2

A Cast of Characters

There are many types of players in the consumer credit game: creditors, credit reporting bureaus, credit repair agencies, the Federal Trade Commission, Congress, and state authorities, not to mention lobbyists at both the state and federal levels. All of them are in the game to make money or protect a means of making it, or to regulate the industry, but none of these players are truly here for you, the individual consumer of credit. Every person who uses credit (more than 90 percent of all American adults) should become familiar with the agencies that influence his or her credit reputations. Knowledge is the first and best avenue to power the individual consumer can have. A brief introduction to the major characters follows, and you will find expanded information in the chapters that follow.

Creditors

For the purposes of this discussion, a creditor is any company, organization, or institution that permits you to use future income to purchase goods and services today. A creditor could be the issuer of a credit card, the company that holds your mortgage, or the bank that helped finance your auto loan. In exchange for advancing you credit to purchase goods or services, creditors expect repayment with interest. Creditors have a keen interest in your payment habits: Will you pay on time? Will you pay the full amount? What have other creditors experienced with you in the past? Many creditors rely on another major player in the credit game (the credit reporting service) to provide them with information about your credit history.

Credit reporting services

There are more than 1,200 credit reporting services in the United States, but there are three in particular that every credit consumer should get to know: Experian, Equifax, and Trans Union. These are national/international agencies that collect credit history information on hundreds of millions of American consumers. This information is provided to them by individual creditors (such as department stores, mortgage companies, and banks), known as subscribers in credit bureau parlance. (Public information, including bankruptcy filings and other legal actions, is also collected by the credit reporting bureaus.) Creditors then purchase complete credit histories on individual consumers from the bureaus. These credit histories are used to evaluate a consumer's creditworthiness when considering extension of credit. Other agencies or individuals may purchase credit information as well, including employers, insurance agencies, and law enforcement agencies.

The three major credit bureaus each have affiliate bureaus that collect credit history information on a more regional basis. These regional agencies enter into a relationship with one of the big three bureaus, with the regional agency storing its information on the national bureau's database. There are also mortgage reporting agencies, which are localized agencies that serve the real estate market and provide credit reports that are a composite of information available through the major credit bureaus.

Experian

Experian, formerly TRW Inc., is based in Orange, Calif. It is one of the nation's largest computerized consumer credit reporting services, maintaining credit information on more than 180 million consumers in the United States. Experian collects and stores that information and provides it to subscribers that have a "permissible purpose" to use it as defined by the Fair Credit Reporting Act (FCRA). Permissible purposes include granting credit, hiring for employment, and underwriting insurance policies. Organizations and companies that subscribe to Experian's service include credit grantors, employers, and insurance underwriters.

Experian entered the credit reporting business when, as TRW, it acquired Credit Data Corporation in 1969. This bureau, originally the Detroit-based Michigan Merchants Credit Association, was founded in 1932. In the early 1960s, the company used file cabinets and three-by-five cards to store consumer credit information. In 1965, Credit Data initiated and installed the first computerized, online credit reporting system. For more than two decades, TRW was the technological leader in the credit reporting industry. It was the first to automate its nationwide database to ensure that consumers' credit histories were kept when they moved or changed their names.

In early 1996, TRW sold its $1.1 billion information businesses to investors led by Bain Capital Inc. and the Thomas H. Lee Co. The company changed its name to Experian. In November 1996, Great Universal Stores PLC purchased Experian and merged it with the CCN Group of Nottingham, United Kingdom, creating a global information leader that is first or second in every market it serves, including the United States, Japan, Australia, France, Germany, the United Kingdom, and more. Experian retains the technological edge it held for so long as TRW.

In return for the credit information and services offered by Experian, subscribers provide Experian with a record of their past and present credit account information, usually on a monthly basis. The regular receipt of this credit information provides Experian with an automatic update of consumer credit account information.

The subscribers' information is typically copied directly from the billing records used to notify customers. Information is sent to Experian's data center in Allen, Texas, where it undergoes a data-verification process before being entered into the company's computer system. Public record information, including bankruptcy filings, is gathered directly from court and county records, converted to a computerized format, and entered into the computer system.

Experian's search and retrieval system can check all areas of the country with a single inquiry. Any previous addresses, alternate surnames (such as maiden names), and nicknames can be retrieved automatically with the current consumer information.

Trans Union

Trans Union, based in Chicago, Ill., is another primary source of credit information, serving a range of industries that routinely evaluate credit risk or verify information about customers. The company's consumer credit information file includes public records information and accounts receivable information from national, regional, and local credit grantors. Trans Union claims that its database includes credit activity information on every credit-active person in the United States.

Equifax

Equifax, based in Atlanta, Ga., operates the largest credit reporting network in the U.S., including company-owned and affiliated credit bureaus. Its annual revenues top $1.6 billion. As with Experian and Trans Union, Equifax offers a variety of information services, but the reporting of credit information is its primary business. Its customers include the nation's largest retailers, banks, and financial institutions, as well as utilities, automobile dealers and rental companies, credit unions, hotels and motels, and others. Its international operations include divisions in Canada, Europe, and South America.

Associated Credit Bureaus

Associated Credit Bureaus (ACB) is a trade association, headquartered in Washington, D.C., with more than 1,450 credit reporting, collection service, and mortgage company members. Its primary functions are legislative affairs, industry operating standards, public relations, and education. ACB serves as a spokesperson for the credit reporting industry with the media and sets voluntary industry standards in addition to providing "legislative support" (lobbying) at the federal and state levels. ACB has been very effective in influencing the amendment of federal law to meet its "industry standards" and preventing adoption of measures favored by consumer advocates that would have limited the amount consumers can be charged to receive copies of their own credit reports.

Credit repair agencies

Credit repair agencies, often called "credit clinics" or "credit doctors," are companies that claim to be able to positively influence your credit rating. They will often claim to have the ability to have negative items removed from your credit by taking advantage of "little-known loopholes in the law." To perform this service they charge a fee, ranging anywhere from $100 to $2,000 or more. Historically, such "businesses" have often been scam operations, skipping town before unwary customers realize their credit ratings are unchanged but their bank balances have dropped. Although some of these businesses are legitimate, no credit repair agency can do any more to affect your report than you can yourself, and no credit agency can remove negative information from your credit report if it is correct. Unfortunately, current conditions in the credit market indicate that many consumers are easy targets for such scams, with more than 70 million consumers having substantially negative credit ratings. (In Chapter 12 I'll explain many of the tactics such agencies use, many of which are illegal, and in Chapter 7 I'll show you how you can repair your own credit.)

The Better Business Bureau

The Better Business Bureau (BBB) was originally founded by Samuel C. Dobbs in 1906 as a vigilance committee to combat unfair advertising practices. Although truth in advertising remains a primary concern for the more than 150 Better Business Bureaus that exist across the country, their mission has expanded to include other programs and goals to make the marketplace a fair and honest place to do business.

The BBB considers the credit repair industry to be one of the most problematic in recent years. Many players in the industry have taken advantage of the poor credit ratings that plague so many consumers. Although there may be legitimate organizations that can help an individual improve or correct credit histories, the industry in general suffers from a well-earned reputation of being a scam. The reason? Unfair and deceptive claims that bad credit can be "erased" or made extinct. These misrepresentations of services—in advertising and sales pitches—have prompted the Better Business Bureau to wage a war on these scam artists through cooperation with law enforcement investigations, advertising challenges, reliability reports to the public, media proposals, and, most importantly, consumer education.

The National Foundation for Consumer Credit

The National Foundation for Consumer Credit is a nonprofit membership organization whose goals are to educate, counsel, and promote the intelligent use of credit in individual and family financial planning. As a national organization, NFCC provides leadership for a growing number—now almost 1,000—of nonprofit community Consumer Credit Counseling Services in the United States and Canada.

Consumer Credit Counseling Services

Consumer Credit Counseling Service (CCCS) is the nation's largest nonprofit organization providing confidential and professional financial and debt counseling to aid and rehabilitate financially distressed customers with debt problems due to job loss, reduced income, divorce, catastrophic illness, or poor financial management. Annually, more than one million people seek the assistance of CCCS, and many of them approach the organization as a last resort to bankruptcy. It is important to note that CCCS, though a nonprofit agency, is largely funded by 10,000 creditors, 31 percent of whom are credit card issuers. CCCS has been beneficial to millions of consumers with credit problems, but it also answers to the creditors, and it rarely recommends bankruptcy, although the conditions may be quite legitimate.

Debt Counselors of America

Debt Counselors of America is another nonprofit organization that assists families and individuals with debt, credit, money, and financial questions, problems, or difficulties. Its services are confidential and are free or available at a low cost. The programs it offers include ONE-PAY, a program in which many creditors will reduce or eliminate interest, stop late charges, bring past due accounts current, and stop collection calls. Debt Counselors of America has taken a high-tech approach, utilizing Internet technology to provide clients with 24-hour access to their accounts on its secure Web site. The Web Account Access System shows the latest amount, date, and transaction number posted for each individual creditor owed, so that clients can monitor and review the progress they are making in repayment of debt.

Chapter 3

Your Credit Report

Across the United States, several thousand credit bureaus collect credit information about consumers. These credit bureaus are connected to centralized computer files that contain data on millions of individuals. Almost instantaneously, a credit bureau can produce for a subscribing creditor a revealing report about your past and present credit activity.

Although they can operate in different ways, many bureaus follow similar procedures. Banks, finance companies, merchants, credit card companies, and other creditors are the paying customers (subscribers) of credit bureaus. Subscribers regularly send credit reports, which contain information about the kind of credit extended, the amount and terms, and the paying habits of individual customers, to the credit bureaus. Some information is collected by the credit bureaus from other sources, such as court records.

What your file may contain

The credit bureau file contains your name, address, Social Security number, and birthdate. A lot of other information also may be included, such as:

- ❑ Your employer, position, and income.
- ❑ Your former address.

- ❑ Your former employer.
- ❑ Your spouse's name, Social Security number, employer, and income.
- ❑ An indication that you own your home, rent, or board.

Your file probably also contains detailed credit information. Each time you buy on credit from a reporting store or take out a loan at a bank, finance company, or other reporting creditor, a credit bureau is informed of your account number as well as the date, amount, terms, and type of credit extended.

As you make payments, your file is updated to show the outstanding balance, the number of payments and amounts past due, and the frequency of 30-, 60- or 90-day lateness. The file also contains public record information about you, including any tax liens, wage garnishments, or legal judgments. Previous late payments, collection actions, and legal judgments can cause a lender to reject your credit application, or can result in higher interest rates and extra finance charges (known as "points") that can make a difference of hundreds (or even thousands) of dollars on a major purchase, such as a car or home. Your record may also indicate the largest amount of credit you've had and the maximum limit permitted by the creditor.

Each time a potential credit grantor reviews your report, it is called an inquiry, and it is recorded as part of the report. The number of inquires on your report can be influential to a potential credit grantor. If there are numerous inquiries without credit having been subsequently extended, then the creditor may conclude that you have been turned down. Often, numerous inquiries are considered ominous by potential creditors, regardless of the outcome.

Requesting your credit report

Copy and use the "Credit Report Request" letter (shown in Chapter 7) to request a copy of your credit report from the major credit reporting agencies listed in this chapter. Be sure to enclose a copy of your driver's license or a credit card bill or utility bill. If you have been denied credit within the past 60 days, you can, by law, receive a free report from the agency that provided the report. Your request must be accompanied by a copy of the denial letter.

Note: Each agency may not have the same information, so you may want to obtain a copy of your report from all of them. As of October 1, 1997, the Fair Credit Reporting Act (FCRA) stipulates that cost to consumers for copies of their credit reports is $8, adjusted annually for inflation, unless otherwise regulated by state law. A few states have lower amounts. Remember: If you have been denied credit, you may request the report at no charge within 60 days.

Experian

P.O. Box 949

Allen, TX 75013

800-682-7654

www.experian.com

Equifax Credit Information Services

P.O. Box 740241

Atlanta, GA 30374-0241

800-685-1111

www.equifax.com

Trans Union Credit Information

Trans Union Consumer Relations

760 West Sproul Road

P.O. Box 390

Springfield, PA 19064-0390

800-851-2674

www.transunion.com

What the credit report says

Credit reports include basic information about consumers, including name, address, Social Security number, marital status, date of birth, spouse's name, number of dependents, previous addresses, and employment information. This is followed by a listing of credit information that includes credit account numbers, creditors' names, the amount of last payment, the credit limit of the account, and the timeliness of credit payments. Some reports contain a listing of public information, including tax liens, court judgments, and bankruptcies. Lastly, there is an inquiry section that notes creditors who have reviewed a copy of the credit report. This section serves as an audit trail for consumers, to ensure that no unauthorized parties have accessed the report.

Unfortunately, if you're like 70 percent of American consumers, you probably have at least one negative item in your credit report. This information may well be incorrect, misleading, inaccurate, or obsolete. Your file could contain information about someone else with a similar name or Social Security number. (The industry term for this is "commingling" of files, and it is a common problem.) Much of the public record information is gathered manually, increasing the odds that it is reported incorrectly in your file.

I recommend that everyone review their credit report annually, regardless of your credit and debt status. Associated Credit Bureaus estimates that two billion pieces of information about consumer trade activity are entered into consumer credit records each month. With that incredible volume, mistakes are bound to happen, and it's in your best interest to catch and correct them before they become a stumbling block in obtaining credit.

Positive, neutral, and negative notations

Information in your report is usually divided into three types of ratings: positive, neutral, and negative.

The following are the only statements in your credit report that are considered positive:

- ❑ Paid satisfactorily or paid as agreed.
- ❑ Current account with no late payments.
- ❑ Account/credit line closed at consumer's request.

The following notations are considered neutral, but in reality, anything less than a positive rating is considered negative by many credit grantors:

- ❑ Paid, was 30 days late.
- ❑ Current, was 30 days late.
- ❑ Inquiry.
- ❑ Credit card lost.
- ❑ Refinance.
- ❑ Settled.
- ❑ Paid.

The following are considered negative:

- ❑ Bankruptcy—Chapter 7 or Chapter 13.
- ❑ Judgments.
- ❑ Liens.
- ❑ Account closed—grantor's request.
- ❑ Paid, was 60, 90, or 120 days late.
- ❑ SCNL (subscriber cannot locate).
- ❑ Paid, collection.
- ❑ Paid, charge-off.
- ❑ Bk liq reo (bankruptcy liquidation).
- ❑ Charge-off.
- ❑ Collection account.
- ❑ Delinquent.
- ❑ Current, was 60, 90, or 120 days late.
- ❑ CHECKPOINT, TRANS ALERT, or CAUTION (potential fraud indicators).
- ❑ Excessive inquiries (looks as if you've been turned down by everyone else).

Credit Scoring

Have you ever wondered how a creditor decides whether to grant you credit? For years, creditors have been using credit scoring systems to determine if you'd be a good risk for credit cards and auto loans. More recently, credit scoring has been used to help creditors evaluate your ability to repay home mortgage loans. Here's how credit scoring works in helping decide who gets credit—and why.

What is credit scoring?

Credit scoring is a system creditors use to help determine whether to give you credit. Information about you and your credit experiences, such as your bill-paying history, the number and type of accounts you have, late payments, collection actions, outstanding debt, and the age of your accounts, is collected from your credit application and your credit report. Using a statistical program, creditors compare this information to the credit performance of consumers with similar profiles. A credit scoring system awards points for each factor that helps predict who is most likely to repay a debt. A total number of points (a credit score) helps predict how creditworthy you are—that is, how likely it is that you will repay a loan and make the payments when due.

Because your credit report is such an important part of many credit scoring systems, it is very important to make sure it's accurate before you submit a credit application.

Why is credit scoring used?

Credit scoring is based on real data and statistics, so it is usually more reliable than subjective or judgmental methods. It treats all applicants objectively. Judgmental methods typically rely on criteria that are not systematically tested and can vary when applied by different individuals.

How is a credit scoring model developed?

To develop a model, a creditor selects a random sample of its customers, or a sample of similar customers if its sample is not large enough, and analyzes it statistically to identify characteristics that relate to creditworthiness. Each of these factors is then assigned a weight based on how strong a predictor it is of who would be a good credit risk. Each creditor may use its own credit scoring model, different scoring models for different types of credit, or a generic model developed by a credit scoring company.

Under the Equal Credit Opportunity Act, a credit scoring system may not use certain characteristics (including race, sex, marital status, national origin, or religion) as factors. However, creditors are allowed to use age in properly designed scoring systems. Any scoring system that includes age must give equal treatment to elderly applicants.

What can I do to improve my score?

Credit scoring models are complex and often vary among creditors and for different types of credit. If one factor changes, your score may change—but improvement generally depends on how that factor relates to other factors considered by the model. Only the creditor can explain what might improve your score under the particular model used to evaluate your credit application.

Nevertheless, scoring models generally evaluate the following types of information in your credit report:

- ❑ **Have you paid your bills on time?** Payment history is typically a significant factor. It is likely that your score will be affected negatively if you have paid bills late, had an account referred to collections, or declared bankruptcy, if that history is reflected on your credit report.
- ❑ **What is your outstanding debt?** Many scoring models evaluate the amount of debt you have compared to your credit limits. If the amount you owe is close to your credit limit, that is likely to have a negative effect on your score.
- ❑ **How long is your credit history?** Generally, models consider the length of your credit track record. An insufficient credit history may have an effect on your

score, but that can be offset by other factors, such as timely payments and low balances.

- ❑ **Have you applied for new credit recently?** Many scoring models consider whether you have applied for credit recently by looking at "inquiries" on your credit report when you apply for credit. If you have applied for too many new accounts recently, that may negatively affect your score. However, not all inquiries are counted. Inquiries by creditors who are monitoring your account or looking at credit reports to make "prescreened" credit offers are not counted.
- ❑ **How many and what types of credit accounts do you have?** Although it is generally good to have established credit accounts, too many credit card accounts may have a negative effect on your score. In addition, many models consider the type of credit accounts you have. For example, under some scoring models, loans from finance companies may negatively affect your credit score.

Scoring models may be based on more than just information in your credit report. For example, the model may consider information from your credit application as well, such as your job or occupation, the length of your employment, or whether you own a home.

To improve your credit score under most models, concentrate on paying your bills on time, paying down outstanding balances, and not taking on new debt. It's likely to take some time to improve your score significantly.

How reliable is the credit scoring system?

Credit scoring systems enable creditors to evaluate millions of applicants consistently and impartially on many different characteristics. To be statistically valid, though, credit scoring systems must be based on a big enough sample. Remember that these systems generally vary from creditor to creditor.

Although you may think such a system is arbitrary or impersonal, it can help make decisions faster, more accurately, and more impartially than individuals when it is properly designed. Many creditors design their systems so that in marginal cases, applicants whose scores are not high enough to pass easily or are low enough to fail absolutely are referred to a credit manager who decides whether the company or lender will extend credit. This may allow for discussion and negotiation between the credit manager and the consumer.

What happens if you are denied credit or don't get the terms you want?

If you are denied credit, the Equal Credit Opportunity Act requires that the creditor give you a notice that tells you the specific reasons your application was rejected or the fact that you have the right to learn the reasons if you ask within 60 days. Indefinite and vague reasons for denial are illegal, so ask the creditor to be specific. Acceptable reasons include: "Your income was low" or "You haven't been employed long enough." Unacceptable reasons include: "You didn't meet our minimum standards" or "You didn't receive enough points on our credit scoring system."

If a creditor says you were denied credit because you are too near your credit limits on your charge cards or you have too many credit card accounts, you may want to reapply after paying down your balances or closing some accounts. Credit scoring systems consider updated information and change over time.

Sometimes you can be denied credit because of information from a credit report. If so, the Fair Credit Reporting Act requires the creditor to give you the name, address, and phone number of the credit reporting agency that supplied the information. You should contact that agency to find out what your report said. This information is free if you request it within 60 days of being turned down for credit. The credit reporting agency can tell you what's in your report, but only the creditor can tell you why your application was denied.

If you've been denied credit, or didn't get the rate or credit terms you want, ask the creditor if a credit scoring system was used.

If so, ask what characteristics or factors were used in that system, and the best ways to improve your application. If you get credit, ask the creditor whether you are getting the best rate and terms available and, if not, why. If you are not offered the best rate available because of inaccuracies in your credit report, be sure to dispute the inaccurate information.

The special status of credit scoring

Although much has been done to regulate credit reports, other products and services provided by credit bureaus (which are information-gathering agencies) are subject to different, fewer, or no regulations. Credit scoring is a service the major bureaus provide to a variety of clients that rates the creditworthiness of individuals based on their credit histories and other types of personal information that may be available. These scores are increasingly being used by creditors to determine whether or not a specific consumer is a good credit risk. In fact, Fannie Mae and Freddie Mac (the nation's largest providers of funding for home mortgages) determined that all applications for mortgages with federal connections must be evaluated using credit scoring by late 1996.

The scores provided by the bureaus are based, at least in part, on the information contained in the credit report (which, as we know, can be wrong). Consumer groups have advocated that the bureaus be required to share the credit score with the consumer. The Federal Trade Commission (FTC), which is charged with enforcing the FCRA, issued a ruling on this question on September 1, 1995. It said, in part:

> The Federal Trade Commission said today that federal law does not require credit bureaus to disclose "risk scores" to consumers who request copies of their credit reports. The FTC reminded consumers, however, that they are still entitled to see their credit reports and to learn from creditors what in their reports led to their denial of credit, if that happens. Today's Commission action follows review of more than 300 pages of public filings in response to the FTC's

> request of last summer for comments on its 1992 interpretation of the Fair Credit Reporting ACT (FCRA), in which the FTC said the FCRA did require disclosure of "risk scores"....

The FCRA, which is enforced by the FTC, gives consumers the right to obtain the nature and substance of all information (except medical information) that is in a credit bureau's files on them at the time they make a request for such information. Because "risk scores" are not in the consumer's file, the FTC concluded that the FCRA did not require disclosure.

Consumer advocates consider this ruling to be a classic case of the tail wagging the watchdog. Though the FTC originally announced it would require disclosure of "risk scores," the credit bureaus succeeded in having the ruling reversed, claiming substantial costs would be associated with providing "risk scores" and asserting that consumers were likely to be confused by the scores rather than benefit from knowing them. The bureaus noted that the FCRA requires a credit bureau to disclose only the "nature and substance of all information...in its files on the consumer at the time of the request" for disclosure by the consumer, but it does not require them to reveal a statistical assessment such as a "risk score" that is not contained in the file.

Chapter 4

Your Rights Under the Fair Credit Reporting Act

For more than 25 years, the Fair Credit Reporting Act (FCRA) has been a primary tool consumers have had available to protect themselves against abuses of the credit reporting system. Congress passed the FCRA in 1971 to regulate the use of credit reports, to require credit bureaus to delete obsolete information, and to give the consumer access to his or her file and the right to have erroneous data corrected. It also placed important limits on the types of persons, businesses, and organizations that can access this very personal information about consumers.

In late 1996, Congress passed legislation updating the law, with most provisions taking effect on October 1, 1997. This chapter summarizes your basic rights under the law, noting those changes that are part of the 1996 update. It's important to familiarize yourself with the law, because mistakes do occur in the credit reporting industry, and such mistakes can affect, sometimes drastically, the lives and livelihoods of responsible citizens.

Limitations on access to information

The FCRA stipulates that a credit report about you may be issued only to properly identified persons for approved purposes. It may be furnished in response to a court order or in accordance with your own written request. It may be provided to someone who will use it in connection with evaluation of a credit transaction, employment, underwriting of insurance, determination of eligibility for a license or other benefit granted by a governmental agency, or other legitimate business need. Friends and neighbors who are curious about your affairs may not obtain information about you. To do so might subject the subscriber who obtained it for them to fine and/or imprisonment.

You, too, may review your file

The FCRA gives you the right to know what your credit file contains, and the credit bureau must provide someone to help you interpret the data. You will be required to identify yourself to the bureau's satisfaction, and you will be charged a fee. There is no fee, however, if you have been turned down for credit, employment, or insurance because of information contained in a report within the preceding 60 days. The credit bureau that reported the adverse information about you is required, by law, to provide you with a copy of your report free of charge. Otherwise the fee is typically $8, unless otherwise stipulated by state law.

The 1996 update to the FCRA expanded the right to receive a free credit report to include the following: unemployed persons who plan to apply for a job within 60 days; persons receiving public assistance (welfare); persons who have been notified by a collection agency affiliated with a credit bureau that a collection action is about to be reported to the bureau; and victims of credit fraud.

Time limits on adverse data

The FCRA states that negative credit history items may only be reported for seven years, which covers most items that would be reported. A significant exception is a declaration of personal bankruptcy, which may be reported for 10 years. (The FCRA does not limit how long positive information can be reported.) After seven years or 10 years, the information can no longer be disclosed by a credit reporting agency, with a few exceptions:

(1) If you are submitting a credit application for $150,000 or more;

(2) If you are seeking to purchase life insurance of $150,000 or more; or

(3) If you are applying for employment at an annual salary of $75,000 or more. In these situations the time limits on releasing negative data do not apply.

The amounts cited here became effective October 1, 1997. Prior to that date, the limits were $50,000 on credit or life insurance applications and $20,000 on employment applications. In addition, the 1996 FCRA update requires that any employer or prospective employer who wishes to pull your credit report (after October 1, 1997) must have your written permission to do so. The request cannot be hidden in small type in an employment application; it must be signed separately. If you are rejected for a job based "in whole or in part" on an item in the credit report, the employer must give you a copy of the report before turning you down as well as written instructions on how to challenge the accuracy of the report.

In spite of these recent changes, it appears that the consumer/job applicant may still have a hard time realizing the benefits of privacy protection. For instance, what is the prospective employer's responsibility to continue consideration of a job candidate if he or she refuses to grant permission to have his credit file accessed? Even if a company does reject a prospective employee based on adverse information in a credit report, what stops the company from claiming a different reason for turning the applicant down? Obviously, it can literally pay to know what's in your credit report. The 1996 FCRA update does provide, however, that credit bureaus must show the name or full trade name of anyone that has requested your credit report in the past year, and for employers, the past two years.

7-year reporting period

There is a standard method for calculating the seven-year reporting period. Generally, the period runs from the date that the event took place.

With regard to any delinquent account placed for collection—internally or by referral to a third-party debt collector, whichever is earlier—charged to profit and loss, or subjected to any similar action, the seven-year period is calculated from the date of the delinquency that occurred immediately before the collection activity, charge to profit and loss, or similar action. For example, assume that your payments on a loan were late in January, but that you caught up in February. You were late again in May, but caught up in July. You were again late in September, but did not catch up before the account was turned over to a collection agency in December. You made no more payments on the account, and it is charged to profit and loss in July of the following year.

Under the FCRA, the January and May late payments each can be reported for seven years. The collection activity and the charge to profit and loss can be reported for seven years from the date of the September payment, which was the delinquency that occurred immediately before those activities.

Accurate negative information

When negative information in your report is accurate, only the passage of time can assure its removal. Accurate negative information generally can stay on your report for seven years. However, there are certain exceptions. These include:

- ❑ Bankruptcy information may be reported for 10 years.
- ❑ Credit information reported in response to an application for a job with a salary of more than $75,000 has no time limit.
- ❑ Information about criminal convictions has no time limit.

- ❑ Credit information reported because of an application for more than $150,000 worth of credit or life insurance has no time limit.
- ❑ Default information concerning U.S. government–insured or guaranteed student loans can be reported for seven years after certain guarantor actions.
- ❑ Information about a lawsuit or an unpaid judgment against you can be reported for seven years or until the statute of limitations runs out, whichever is longer.

Adding accounts to your file

Your credit file may not reflect all your credit accounts. Although most national department store and all-purpose bank credit card accounts will be included in your file, not all creditors supply information to CRAs. Some travel, entertainment, and gasoline card companies, as well as local retailers and credit unions, are among those creditors that don't.

If you've been told that you were denied credit because of an "insufficient credit file" or "no credit file" and you have accounts with creditors that don't appear in your credit file, ask the CRA to add this information to future reports. Although they are not required to do so, many CRAs will add verifiable accounts for a fee. Understand that if these creditors do not report to the CRA on a regular basis, the added items will not be updated in your file.

Incorrect information

Credit bureaus are required to follow reasonable procedures to ensure that subscribing creditors report information accurately. However, mistakes often occur. Your file may contain erroneous data or records of someone with a name or Social Security number similar to yours. When you notify the credit bureau that you dispute the accuracy of information, the bureau is required to reinvestigate within 30 days and, if necessary, modify or remove inaccurate data. Any pertinent information you have concerning an error should be given to the credit bureau. The bureau may not charge you for this reinvestigation. Within five business days of completing the investigation, results must be sent to the consumer, along with a copy of the credit report. The new law also requires that corrected information must be shared among the major credit bureaus.

The credit bureau turns to the reporting agency (the creditor) to verify disputed information. If the information cannot be verified within the 30-day time limit, it must be deleted. The 1996 FCRA update stipulates that if the creditor verifies the information at a later date, negative information can be reinserted to the file, and the credit bureau must notify the consumer. A creditor cannot knowingly provide incorrect information. If it has made a mistake, it is required to notify all major credit bureaus to which it has reported the incorrect information.

Adding your own statement to the file

If reinvestigation does not resolve the dispute to your satisfaction, you may enter a statement of 100 words or less into your file explaining why you think the record is inaccurate. The law, however, does not require a credit bureau to add to your credit file a statement of circumstances that explains a period of delinquency caused by some unexpected hardship, such as serious illness, a catastrophe, or unemployment, which eliminated or drastically reduced your income. This type of explanation should be given by you directly to a credit grantor when applying for credit.

The credit bureau is required to include your statement about disputed data—or a coded version of it—with any reports it issues about you. At your request, the bureau must also send a correction to anyone who received a report in the preceding six months if it was for a credit check, or within a two-year period if it was for employment purposes. Under the 1996 FCRA update, you can be charged for this, but no more than the creditor would be charged to receive the information.

High-tech credit relief

In addition to new legislation, technological advances have made it easier and faster for consumers to fight credit-report errors and update their report. Until recently, consumers who disputed, say, an entry about a credit card account have had to send separate letters to the three national credit bureaus (Equifax, Trans Union, and Experian). The bureaus, in turn, would ask the creditor that supplied the questionable data to verify the items, which could take 30 days or more. Credit bureaus and creditors now use the Automated Consumer Dispute Verification (ACDV) system that automatically reports errors to all the major bureaus. Previously, credit bureaus and creditors mailed paper copies of such data to one another.

The ACDV system was adopted voluntarily by the three major credit bureaus and major creditors, and it appears it will be the mechanism used to comply with the new requirement that changes in reported information must be automatically shared by the bureaus.

Chapter 5

The Importance of Good Credit

A person with "good credit" manages credit well and pays bills on time. Good credit and a healthy credit rating are more important now than in the past.

Here's why: Today you need good credit to get more credit. If you want to buy a house or a car, get a college loan for your child's education, or simply apply for a credit card, the bank or credit union will check your credit report. An insurance company will check your report if you apply for more insurance.

Good credit is convenient for consumers and businesses. In fact, many businesses strongly prefer the use of credit cards. For instance, it's very difficult to rent a car or hotel room without a credit card. Because of these policies, most people should probably consider obtaining at least one credit card. (If you do not handle credit well, however, you may not want to get one. A credit card is useful, but it may make matters worse for some people.)

More and more employers are checking the credit ratings of prospective employees. Not all employers check, but those that do look unfavorably on a negative credit rating.

Available credit is helpful for unplanned situations and emergencies. Having good credit does not mean being in debt. Rather, it means having the unused capacity to obtain credit. Credit capacity is useful for convenience, emergencies, and unplanned bills. You may have a regular income and always pay your bills on time. Unfortunately, this doesn't equal a good credit rating.

Reasons for denial of credit

You may be denied credit because of an "insufficient credit history." That may indicate you are just starting out in the world of credit. Perhaps you are very young, or you have experienced a major change in your life circumstances, such as death or divorce. Or it may simply mean that your lifetime of bill payments is not recorded in the computers that make up today's credit system. You may have paid your bills on a cash basis instead of with credit cards. Your credit may have been with local banks, credit unions, and department stores that do not report monthly mortgage or loan payments to credit bureaus. So even though you've used credit all your life, you could apply for new credit and find that your credit report is blank. In any case, a lack of credit history can hurt your application.

You may be denied credit because your credit report is mixed up with someone else's. Your personal credit history may be on your credit report and reflect positively, but your credit report may list the bad parts of someone else's credit history, too.

You may be denied credit because of your age, race, or marital status. According to the Equal Credit Opportunity Act, it is illegal to discriminate on the basis of age, race, or marital status, but it can happen. Many divorced and widowed women report special credit problems. When they were married, their credit was in their spouses' names rather than their own; their own credit histories are a blank.

Finally, some banks or other lenders may illegally discount nonsalary income. The Equal Credit Opportunity Act requires creditors who consider sources of income to consider Social Security, child support, and alimony equally with employment income.

Causes of poor credit

Most adult American consumers have at least one negative item on their credit report. In some cases, these negative items are inaccurate or misleading. Such inaccuracies can be caused by clerical errors, mistaken identities, or fraud. In some cases you may find accounts that you believe to have been current (paid) reflecting an unpaid or delinquent status. In other cases, you may find accounts or other information that belong to someone else with a similar name. This is especially common with Juniors and Seniors in the same household.

Most of the time, however, the information found on your credit report will reflect your payment history for various accounts over the last several years. In light of the rising divorce rate, corporate downsizing, economic recessions, and problems with healthcare insurance systems, many individuals have found themselves unable to make ends meet at one time or another. Many of us have suffered medical problems, job layoffs, or other temporary setbacks that caused us to fall behind on our bills for a period of time. Unfortunately, such setbacks may continue to haunt us for years to come in the form of negative information on our credit reports.

Another major cause of poor credit is poor judgment. Many consumers overextend themselves with credit cards, signature loans, high car payments, second mortgages, and overdraft checking privileges. Before they know it, they are over their heads in debt and unable to make all of their payments. In the most extreme cases, individuals have found themselves in bankruptcy court, in small claims court, or facing foreclosure. These "public record" items can be even more damaging to a credit rating.

Some of us are simply poor money managers. In spite of having more than enough income to cover monthly expenses, many individuals simply forget to pay all of their bills on time or neglect to mail them before the due date. As a result their credit reports are littered with late payments, delinquencies, and collection accounts.

Many people today are faced with personal financial problems. And things can look bleak when you're burdened with bills that add up to more than you earn each month. The reasons for financial problems are, of course, as various as the people who experience them: a loss or reduction in income, a change in marital status, or unexpected or emergency expenses. There's also the ready availability of credit itself. Credit can be so convenient that it's tempting to use too much of it.

Whether it's the result of inaccurate information in your files or poor decisions in the past, a negative credit rating can cause you much hardship and humiliation. Remember, in any case, that you are not alone. More than 40 million American adults are rejected for credit each year.

If you are rejected for credit, take the necessary action toward repairing your credit. In the next chapters you will learn a simple approach to repairing your credit if inaccurately reported, or reestablishing your credit—regardless of your present situation.

Chapter 6

7 Steps to Reestablishing Your Credit

Your creditworthiness influences not only whether you can obtain a loan or purchase goods and services on credit, but it may also affect your employment, living accommodations, or obtaining insurance. If you have a poor credit history, it will take time for you to regain your credibility with credit grantors. You must be able to show that in spite of previous debt problems, you can now handle credit in a financially responsible manner. To assist in this process, here are seven steps you can follow.

Step 1: Pay off your debts.

No matter how you got into credit trouble, it will help to restore your credit if you can bring your debt balance to zero. Lenders generally look more favorably on individuals who have solved debt problems than those who ignore them.

Begin by developing a liquidation plan to repay your debts. Make a list of all your debts so that you have a clear picture of your financial situation. Develop a repayment strategy; determine how much you can repay each month until you have paid off what you owe. Then, pay your bills on time. In my book *Life Without Debt*, I explain the concept of a master repayment strategy in detail, offering insights into targeting which bills to repay first to get you out of debt with maximum efficiency.

Another excellent source of budgeting advice and assistance in developing a realistic repayment schedule is the Consumer Credit Counseling Service (CCCS). This nonprofit organization offers confidential counseling, assisting consumers with financial or debt management. (Bear in mind, however, that CCCS is largely funded by creditors, and it rarely recommends bankruptcy. Although bankruptcy is an extreme measure that should be avoided if possible, there are cases in which it is legitimate. See Chapter 10 for more information.) To find the office closest to you, call its referral number (800-388-CCCS).

Other sources of assistance include your local law school and your local legal aid society, which can provide you with referrals to attorneys specializing in debt reorganization and negotiated settlement. The assistance of a competent legal professional is highly recommended for dealing with such issues as bankruptcy, the IRS, and student loan administration settlements.

Step 2: Design a plan to manage your money.

Often people develop financial problems because they overextend their credit use. In order to reduce the likelihood that you will find yourself in a credit crunch again and help you reduce debt, analyze your spending habits, create financial goals, and set spending priorities.

Step 3: Pay with cash.

Even if you have credit available, you are more likely to change your spending habits by not using it. When you pay with cash or even a check, it forces you to recognize that the money you can spend is limited to the amount of funds you have in your checking account. Debit cards also serve this purpose, because the amount you spend is immediately deducted from your account. You will need to make choices about what you can afford to buy, and therefore you will have to determine your priorities. This sort of forced discipline should eventually enable you to better manage credit.

Step 4: Obtain your credit report.

Most credit bureaus are part of one of the "Big Three" automated reporting systems: Experian, Equifax, or Trans Union. After you have been denied credit because of negative information, you may obtain a free copy of your credit report from the bureau that supplied the information. The bureaus will allow you up to 60 days to make this request. Again, because each report is different, you should check your credit history in all three systems.

If you believe that there is an error in your file, you can write the credit bureau and fill out a dispute form. The bureau will verify the information with the creditor to insure that it is correct. If it is found to be an error, or if the information can no longer be verified, it should be removed from your report. The credit bureau is required by law to share the corrected information with the other bureaus. If the creditor states that the questioned item is accurate, and after you inform the creditor in writing that there is still a disagreement, you may submit a written statement of less than 100 words explaining the dispute to the credit bureau that will become part of your record.

Step 5: Apply for secured credit.

If you are trying to reestablish credit (or establish credit for the first time), one measure to consider is to obtain secured credit. Credit is secured when something of value is pledged to assure loan repayment, or if the responsibility for repayment is shared with a proven creditworthy individual.

One place to start to gain secured credit is access to credit cardholder privileges through your parents or spouse. You may also have a relative or friend who will co-sign a loan. Other options for reestablishing your credit reputation with secured credit include providing an "enhanced down payment" for something (perhaps as much as 50 percent of the purchase price of an item) or by opening an account with a utility in your name. If you do not have telephone, gas, or electricity service in your name, you may try to open accounts with these companies. By providing a security deposit, you may be able to obtain this form of credit and establish an on-time payment history.

If you have a savings account at a bank or credit union, you may be able to obtain a signature loan (that is, borrow a small amount using the savings account as collateral). Some banks will issue you a secured credit card. With a secured credit card, you will be required to put a deposit in the bank, in the form of a certificate of deposit or savings account. In exchange, you obtain a credit line, usually equal to one-and-a-half times the amount of your deposit. The deposit is frozen by the bank and acts as collateral from which the bank can draw if you do not pay on time. However, remember that in addition, as with any credit application, you often will be required to have a minimum salary and minimum length of residence to be accepted for secured credit.

In the past couple of years, a number of major banks have launched secured cards. Interest rates on secured cards, which used to be 21 percent and higher, have fallen; some are now as low as their unsecured counterparts. Because of the attached deposit, banks are assured of recovering their loans. As a result, some banks are now willing to offer secured cards to customers who have been through bankruptcy.

It is important to understand that secured cards are treated exactly as regular credit cards are. For instance, businesses cannot tell that your account is secured by looking at the card or by phoning in for authorization. By the same token, if you fail to make payments on the card, you will be subject to a collection procedure. In other words, the bank will not simply deduct payments from your frozen collateral as they might with overdraft protection. The deposit will be seized as a last resort, only when you or the bank cancels the account and your bills remain unpaid.

Step 6: Apply for unsecured credit.

A local department store may be more likely to issue you a charge card than a national creditor. If you can offer a reasonable explanation for your past credit behavior and show that you are now financially responsible, this information may help. Once you obtain a charge card and pay your bills promptly for a reasonable length of time, your credit line will probably be increased. If you cannot get a department store card, you may be able to begin by purchasing an item on a layaway plan. When you show that you are reliable, the store will be more inclined to provide you with a charge card.

It is important, however, that you limit your credit applications to few stores, because each application will create a creditor inquiry that will likely appear on your credit report. Too many inquiries may cause creditors to think you are applying for more credit than you can afford, causing them to reject your application.

Step 7: Continue to educate yourself.

The credit system is extremely intricate and constantly changing. Every year, millions of Americans are caught up in a web of overwhelming debt and confusion. The rising level of personal debt, coupled with the introduction of dozens of new products in the credit marketplace, makes the need for timely, complete, and user-friendly consumer education greater than ever.

Read as many books as you can find on consumer credit and personal finance. To save money, visit your local library. Increased awareness of the system will help you to guard against repeating mistakes in the future. As you continue to educate yourself, you will also increase your confidence in your ability to become master of your own financial destiny.

These simple steps, when diligently put into action, will dramatically improve your credit status, regardless of your present situation. The important thing is to begin now by putting these ideas into practice in your daily life.

For additional information or assistance, refer to the publications and resources listed in Appendix B.

Chapter 7

Repairing Your Credit Step-by-step

There's a brisk business among credit repair companies that charge from $50 to more than $1,000 to "fix" your credit report. In the past these outfits have taken money and done little or nothing to improve credit reports. Often they just vanished. Be wary of credit repair companies that guarantee to clean up your credit report. Such promises cannot be kept unless the information in your credit report is actually wrong or out of date.

Remember, too, that if there are genuine mistakes or outdated information in your report, you can fix them yourself. In fact, you can do anything a credit repair company can do—for free or for only a few dollars.

Disputing items on your credit report

The first step in repairing your credit is knowing exactly what your credit report says. If you have been denied credit within the past 60 days, you have the right to receive a free copy of your credit report from the bureau that provided negative information. However, I recommend a proactive approach; I believe every consumer should regularly (annually to every three years) review his or her credit reports from each of the Big Three bureaus: Experian, Equifax, and Trans Union.

According to the Fair Credit Reporting Act (FCRA), you have the right to dispute any remark on your report that you "reasonably believe" to be inaccurate or incomplete. The act requires the credit bureau to reinvestigate those disputed items within "a reasonable period of time," interpreted by the Federal Trade Commission as 30 days. If the bureau finds that the information was incorrect, obsolete, or could no longer be verified, it must correct or delete the information.

How to dispute

Obtain a credit report and analyze the report for items you believe to be inaccurate, incomplete, or obsolete. For example, you thought you owed $800 on your Visa card account. The account is presently under collection, but your credit report shows a balance of $900. This is inaccurate, and you have the right to dispute the entire account.

Send the bureau a dispute form (one should be enclosed with your credit report). If you don't have a consumer dispute form, follow the example at the end of this chapter. Be sure to include the items you are disputing, the names of the creditors (subscribers), and the account numbers. Indicate why you believe the item is being reported incorrectly (for example, the amount owed is incorrect, the account is not yours, the account has been paid in full, the number of late payments is incorrect, etc.).

Keep track of the date the dispute was sent. If you do not receive a response within six weeks, immediately send a follow-up letter (see the sample at the end of this chapter).

Obtain results of the credit bureau's reinvestigation. Most credit bureaus will notify you of the result of the investigation and send you a copy of your updated credit report.

Keep a record of all correspondence. Make copies of all credit reports, disputes, replies, and responses. If the reply is by telephone, note the date and time of the call, the name of the person you spoke with, and the nature of the conversation.

Chances are, once you dispute an item, you will receive a response within six weeks, but there have been many instances where bureaus have dragged their feet or lost track of disputes. If the bureau does not respond to your initial dispute within a "reasonable time," follow up promptly. This time, insist that the bureau respond to your dispute immediately. Give them about four weeks to comply and, again, be sure to maintain copies of all correspondence.

If the bureau persists in violating your rights by refusing to reinvestigate your legitimate dispute, send them a final letter demanding action. This time, threaten to take legal action, and send copies of your letter, along with the original request, to the Federal Trade Commission and to your local office of the attorney general.

Sample statements of dispute

Under the Fair Credit Reporting Act, you have the right to add to your credit report a statement of up to 100 words regarding any item(s) you wish to clarify. This statement will then appear on all subsequent reports sent to your credit grantors. Here are some examples:

- "This is not my account. I have never owed money to this creditor. Apparently, a mistake was made in the reporting."
- "On (date), I moved to another address. I notified all creditors, including (name of creditor) promptly. (Name of creditor) was slow in changing my address in its file. Subsequently, I did not receive my billing statement for (how long). Once I received the statement at my new address, I paid this creditor."
- "On (date), I was hospitalized at (facility). The medical bills were forwarded to my insurance company for payment. My insurance company delayed in paying and the hospital turned my account over for collection. Afterwards, my insurance company paid the hospital

bill in full. The hospital's collection agency refused, however, to change the negative rating of my account."

- "This account belongs to my former spouse. My name is no longer on this account."
- "On (date), I ordered merchandise from (name of company) on my account. The merchandise was defective, and I returned it to the sender. The company continued to send me a bill for the returned defective merchandise. The company went out of business before I was able to have my account properly credited."

Questions and answers about credit reports

Q: How will the credit bureau respond to my dispute?

A: The credit reporting agency may respond with one of the following answers:

- "We have changed your credit file as requested."
- "Your credit file will not be changed because (reason)."
- "The party involved did not respond, so the information is being removed by reason of default."

Q: What if the response is no change to the report?

A: You have the right to request that the information be reinvestigated or you can place a 100-word statement of dispute in your report.

Q: How is bankruptcy reported to the credit bureaus?

A: Bankruptcy will show up on your credit report as a public record and may remain on your report for up to 10 years. Each account included in the bankruptcy will show up on your credit report as either a "chargeoff" or a "bankruptcy liquidation."

Q: Are there any positive items that can show up on a credit report?

A: Other than your identifying information, such as name and address, the only positive remarks on a credit report will be for accounts that are either "paid satisfactorily" or "current account with no late payments." Nonrated items may include inquiries, accounts closed by consumer request, or refinance. Other items on a credit report are usually negative, such as late payments, collection accounts, chargeoffs, tax liens, repossessions, foreclosure, and so forth.

Q: How can public record items be removed from a credit report?

A: If the item is incorrect, misleading, or obsolete it can be disputed. If the bureau cannot verify the disputed information, it must be deleted from your credit report. If a lien or judgment has already been paid, but the report reflects it as being unpaid, you should contact the original creditor and request a discharge form. That discharge form is then submitted to the court clerk to be recorded, and a copy of the recorded document is sent to the credit bureau as evidence that the lien or judgment has been satisfied.

Q: Do consumers have the right to ask that their accounts not be sent for collection?

A: Yes. If you are late in paying on your account, you should contact the creditor and ask to make an alternative payment plan. In some cases, you may be able to make reduced monthly payments or "skip" a payment without being penalized. In other cases (such as with an account that has already been charged off) you may be able to negotiate a settlement payment with the creditor.

Consumer statements

Under the Fair Credit Reporting Act, you have the right to add to your credit report a statement of up to 100 words regarding any item(s) you wish to clarify. This statement, or a version of it, will then appear on all subsequent reports sent to your credit grantors.

The consumer statement has often proven to be a very effective tool, especially if the amount of the negative account is small or if you have many positive items to cover a single negative. Here are some examples of consumer statements:

- ❑ "Attention. Apparently someone has been using my identification to obtain credit. Please verify with me at (phone number) prior to the extension of new credit."
- ❑ "Attention. This is not my account. I have never owed money to this creditor. Apparently, a mistake was made during reporting."
- ❑ "During the period from (beginning date) to (ending date), I was laid off work without advance notice. I have always paid my creditors promptly and satisfactorily prior to and since that period. I am now gainfully employed and have been with the same employer since (starting date)."

Disputing with creditors

Another avenue to repairing credit is to deal directly with the creditors that are reporting negative information about you to the credit bureaus. Creditors have the authority to change or delete items from your credit report. The first step in resolving such matters is to make sure that the reported item is correct and properly documented. If you believe the creditor delivered substandard service, sold you defective merchandise, misplaced your check, failed to deliver goods, or otherwise did not perform its part of the agreement, you can dispute the item in the same way described for disputing with credit bureaus. A sample letter of dispute (that can be modified to fit your specific situation) is included at the end of this chapter.

If the debt reported by the creditor is yours, you should attempt to satisfy it, while at the same time negotiating to have the item removed from your credit report. You may offer from 70 percent to the full amount in repayment, in exchange for the removal of the negative item from your report. It is very important that the creditor's representative you work with has the power to authorize such an agreement, so do not hesitate to speak with a supervisor.

Negotiation strategies vary greatly depending upon the debt incurred and creditor you are dealing with (negotiating with a bank over loan repayment is quite different than negotiating with a department store over late payments, for example). Many companies already have special programs in place for allowing consumers to skip a payment during times of financial crisis. Some will allow you to make interest-only payments for several months while deferring the principal amount you owe. For complex negotiations, especailly those involving real estate, taxes, or pending lawsuits, get an attorney's advice. (This subject is covered in detail in my book *Life After Debt.)*

For more information

The FTC enforces several federal laws involving consumer credit. These include the Equal Credit Opportunity Act, the Fair Credit Billing Act, and the Fair Debt Collection Practices Act. For single free copies of brochures about these laws or related publications entitled Solving Credit Problems, Women and Credit Histories, Credit Billing Errors, or How to Dispute Credit Report Errors, write or call: Public Reference, FTC, Washington, D.C. 20580; (202) 326-2222. TDD: (202) 326-2502. You can also visit the FTC's Web site at *www. ftc.gov.*

Sample Credit Report Request

Date
Name of credit bureau
Address of credit bureau
City, State ZIP

Please send me a copy of my credit report.

My full name is: (Jr./Sr./etc.)
My Social Security number is:
My date of birth is:
My address is:
Previous address (last five years):

I may have received credit in the last five years under the following names (e.g. maiden name, etc.):

Enclosed is a copy of a recent billing statement (or driver's license) as proof of my name and address.

(If applicable) I am making this request for a free credit report since I have been denied credit in the last 60 days based on one of your reports. A copy of the denial letter is attached for your information.

(If applicable) A check or money order for $8 is enclosed.*

Sincerely,

(your name)

*This fee pertains to credit reports if you have not been denied credit within the last 60 days. Some states mandate lower fees.

Sample Letter of Credit Report Dispute

Date
Name of agency
Attn.: Consumer Relations
Re: (your name)
(your ID#)
(your address)
(your telephone number)
(your Social Security number)
(your date of birth)

Please begin an investigation of the following items listed on my credit report that do not belong in my credit file.

Company's name	Account #	Reason for dispute
____________	____________	____________
____________	____________	____________
____________	____________	____________

Please update my credit report and send me a copy at the conclusion of your investigation. Send the results to the following organizations that have reviewed my credit report in the past six months and/or to employers that have reviewed it during the past two years.

Thank you for your help and prompt attention to this matter.

Respectfully,

(your name)

Sample Follow-up Letter to a Credit Report Dispute

Date

Name of credit bureau
Address of credit bureau
City, State ZIP

Attn.: Consumer Relations Department

To whom it may concern:

On (date of first dispute), I sent you a request to investigate certain items on my credit report that I believed to be incorrect or inaccurate. As of today, six weeks have passed, and I have not yet received a response from you. Under the Fair Credit Reporting Act, you are required to respond "within a reasonable time." If the information cannot be verified, please delete it from my credit report. I would appreciate your immediate attention to this matter and your informing me of the result.

Yours sincerely,

(your name)
(your address)
(your Social Security number)
(your date of birth)

Sample Second Follow-up Letter to a Credit Report Dispute

Date

Name of credit bureau
Address of credit bureau
City, State ZIP

Re: (your name)
(your address)
(your Social Security number)

Four weeks ago I sent a follow-up letter stating that you had neither responded to nor investigated my disputes of certain incorrect items found on my credit report. Copies of that letter and of the original dispute are enclosed.

You still have not complied with your obligation under the Fair Credit Reporting Act, which requires your company to ensure the correctness of reported information.

I demand that you immediately remove the disputed items from my credit file based on the fact that they are either inaccurate or unverifiable. I also expect you to send me an updated copy of my report immediately afterward.

If I do not receive your response within the next two weeks, I will file a complaint with the Federal Trade Commission and the state attorney general. In addition, I will not hesitate to retain my attorney to pursue my right to recover damages under the Fair Credit Reporting Act.

Please forward me the names and addresses of individuals you contacted to verify the information so I may follow up. Thank you for your immediate attention to this matter.

Sincerely yours,

(your name)

Sample Dispute Letter to a Creditor

Date

Name of creditor

Address of creditor

City, State ZIP

Re: (your name)
(your address)
(your account number)

To whom it may concern:

I have recently obtained a credit report from (credit bureau). It shows the above account with your company was (number) days late (or it has been charged off, etc.). According to the best of my recollection, I have always paid this account promptly and satisfactorily. This incorrect information is highly injurious to my credit rating. I would appreciate it if you would verify this information and correct it with the above-named credit bureau immediately. If the information cannot be verified, please delete the account from my credit report.

Please inform me as to the result of your verification as soon as possible. Your immediate attention to this matter is greatly appreciated.

Sincerely yours,

(your name)

Chapter 8

Credit Card Secrets

Pre-approved credit card offers

Chances are you've gotten your share of "pre-approved" credit card offers in the mail, some with low introductory rates and other perks. Many of these solicitations urge you to accept "before the offer expires." Before you accept, shop around to get the best deal.

Credit card terms

A credit card is a form of borrowing that often involves charges. Credit terms and conditions affect your overall cost, so it's wise to compare terms and fees before you agree to open a credit or charge card account. The following are some important terms to consider that generally must be disclosed in credit card applications or in solicitations that require no application. You also may want to ask about these terms when you're shopping for a card.

Annual Percentage Rate (APR). The APR is a measure of the cost of credit, expressed as a yearly rate. It also must be disclosed before you become obligated on the account and on your account statements.

The card issuer also must disclose the periodic rate, which is the rate applied to your outstanding balance to figure the finance charge for each billing period.

Some credit card plans allow the issuer to change your APR when interest rates or other economic indicators (called indexes) change. Because the rate change is linked to the index's performance, these plans are called "variable rate" programs. Rate changes raise or lower the finance charge on your account. If you're considering a variable rate card, the issuer must also provide various information that discloses to you:

- That the rate may change; and
- How the rate is determined—in other words, which index is used and what additional amount (called the margin) is added to determine your new rate.

You also must receive information, before you become obligated on the account, about any limitations on how much and how often your rate may change.

Free period. Also called a "grace period," a free period lets you avoid finance charges by paying your balance in full before the due date. Knowing whether a card gives you a free period is especially important if you plan to pay your account in full each month. Without a free period, the card issuer may impose a finance charge from the date you use your card or from the date each transaction is posted to your account. If your card includes a free period, the issuer must mail your bill at least 14 days before the due date so you'll have enough time to pay.

Annual fees. Most issuers charge annual membership or participation fees. They often range from $25 to $50, sometimes up to $100; "gold" or "platinum" cards often charge up to $75 and sometimes up to several hundred dollars.

Transaction fees and other charges. A card may include other costs. Some issuers charge a fee if you use the card to get a cash advance, make a late payment, or exceed your credit limit. Some charge a monthly fee whether or not you use the card.

Balance computation method for the finance charge. If you don't have a free period, or if you expect to pay for purchases over time, it's important to know what method the issuer uses to calculate your finance charge. This can make a big difference in how much of a finance charge you'll pay—even if the APR and your buying patterns remain relatively constant. Examples of balance computation methods include the following:

- **Average daily balance.** This is the most common calculation method. It credits your account from the day payment is received by the issuer. To figure the balance due, the issuer totals the beginning balance for each day in the billing period and subtracts any credits made to your account that day. Although new purchases may or may not be added to the balance, depending on your plan, cash advances typically are included. The resulting daily balances are added for the billing cycle. The total is then divided by the number of days in the billing period to get the average daily balance.
- **Adjusted balance.** This is usually the most advantageous method for card holders. Your balance is determined by subtracting payments or credits received during the current billing period from the balance at the end of the previous billing period. Purchases made during the billing period aren't included.

  This method gives you until the end of the billing cycle to pay a portion of your balance to avoid the interest charges on that amount. Some creditors exclude prior, unpaid finance charges from the previous balance.
- **Previous balance.** This is the amount you owed at the end of the previous billing period. Payments, credits, and new purchases during the current billing period are not included. Some creditors also exclude unpaid finance charges.
- **Two-cycle balances.** Issuers sometimes use various methods to calculate your balance that make use of your last two months' account activity. Read your agreement carefully to find out if your issuer uses this approach and, if so, what specific two-cycle method is used.

If you don't understand how your balance is calculated, ask your card issuer. An explanation must also appear on your billing statements.

Other costs and features

Credit terms vary among issuers. When shopping for a card, think about how you plan to use it. If you expect to pay your bills in full each month, the annual fee and other charges may be more important than the periodic rate and the APR, if there is a grace period for purchases. However, if you use the cash advance feature, many cards do not permit a grace period for the amounts due (even if they have a grace period for purchases). So, it may still be wise to consider the APR and balance computation method. If you plan to pay for purchases over time, the APR and the balance computation method are definitely major considerations.

You'll probably also want to consider whether the credit limit is high enough, how widely the card is accepted, and what the plan's services and features are. For example, you may be interested in "affinity cards," all-purpose credit cards sponsored by professional organizations, college alumni associations, and some members of the travel industry. An affinity card issuer often donates a portion of the annual fees or charges to the sponsoring organization, qualifies you for free travel, or offers other bonuses.

Also consider special delinquency rates. Some cards with low rates for on-time payments apply a very high APR if you are late a certain number of times in any specified time period. These rates sometimes exceed 20 percent. Information about delinquency rates should be disclosed to you in credit card applications or in solicitations that do not require an application.

Receiving a credit card

Federal law prohibits issuers from sending you a card you didn't ask for. However, an issuer can send you a renewal or substitute card without your request. Issuers also may send you an application or a solicitation, or ask you by phone if you want a card. If you say yes, they may send you one.

Cardholder protections

Federal law protects your use of credit cards. This includes:

Prompt credit for payment. An issuer must credit your account the day payment is received. The exceptions are if the payment is not made according to the creditor's requirements or the delay in crediting your account won't result in a charge.

To help avoid finance charges, follow the issuer's mailing instructions. Payments sent to the wrong address could delay crediting your account for up to five days. If you misplace your payment envelope, look for the payment address on your billing statement or call the issuer.

Refunds of credit balances. When you make a return or pay more than the total balance at present, you can keep the credit on your account or write your issuer for a refund, as long as it's more than a dollar. A refund must be issued within seven business days of receiving your request. If a credit stays on your account for more than six months, the issuer must make a good faith effort to send you a refund.

Errors on your bill. Issuers must follow rules for promptly correcting billing errors. You'll get a statement outlining these rules when you open an account and at least once a year. In fact, many issuers include a summary of these rights on your bills.

If you find a mistake on your bill, you can dispute the charge and withhold payment on that amount while the charge is being investigated. The error might be a charge for the wrong amount, for something you didn't accept, or for an item that wasn't delivered as agreed. Of course, you still have to pay any part of the bill that's not in dispute, including finance and other charges.

If you decide to dispute a charge:

- ❑ Write to the creditor at the address indicated on your statement for "billing inquiries." Include your name, address, account number, and a description of the error.

- ❑ Send your letter soon. It must reach the creditor within 60 days after the first bill containing the error was mailed to you.

The creditor must acknowledge your complaint in writing within 30 days of receipt, unless the problem has been resolved. At the latest, the dispute must be resolved within two billing cycles, but not more than 90 days.

Unauthorized charges. If your card is used without your permission, you can be held responsible for up to $50 per card.

If you report the loss before the card is used, you can't be held responsible for any unauthorized charges. If a thief uses your card before you report it missing, the most you'll owe for unauthorized charges is $50.

To minimize your liability, report the loss as soon as possible. Most issuers have 24-hour toll-free telephone numbers to accept emergency information. It's a good idea to follow up with a letter to the issuer that includes your account number, the date you noticed your card missing, and the date you reported the loss.

Disputes about merchandise or services. You can dispute charges for unsatisfactory goods or services. To do so, you must:

- ❑ Have made the purchase in your home state or within 100 miles of your current billing address. The charge must be for more than $50. (These limitations don't apply if the seller also is the card issuer or if a special business relationship exists between the seller and the card issuer.)
- ❑ First make a good faith effort to resolve the dispute with the seller. No special procedures are required to do so.

If these conditions don't apply, you may want to consider filing an action in small claims court.

Shopping tips

Keep these tips in mind when looking for a credit or charge card.

- ❑ Shop around for the plan that best fits your needs.
- ❑ Make sure you understand a plan's terms before you accept the card.
- ❑ Pay bills promptly to keep finance and other charges to a minimum.
- ❑ Hold on to receipts to reconcile charges when your bill arrives.
- ❑ Protect your cards and account numbers to prevent unauthorized use. Draw a line through blank spaces on charge slips so the amount can't be changed. Tear up carbons.
- ❑ Keep a record—in a safe place separate from your cards—of your account numbers, expiration dates, and the phone numbers of each issuer to report a loss quickly.
- ❑ Carry only the cards you think you'll use.

Credit card blocking

Have you ever been told you were over your credit limit, even though you knew you weren't? If this happened shortly after you stayed in a hotel or rented a car, the problem could have been credit card "blocking."

What is blocking?

When you use a credit or charge card to check into a hotel or rent a car, the clerk usually contacts the company that issued your card to give an estimated total. If the transaction is approved, your available credit is reduced by this amount. That's a block.

Here's how it works: Suppose you use a credit card when you check into a $100-per-night hotel for five nights. At least $500 would be blocked. In addition, hotels and rental car companies sometimes include anticipated charges for incidentals, such as food, beverages, or gasoline. These amounts can vary widely among merchants.

If you pay your bill with the same card you used when you checked in, the final charge probably will replace the block in a day or two. However, if you pay your bill with a different card, or with cash or a check, the company that issued the card you used at check-in might hold the block for up to 15 days after you've checked out. That's because they weren't notified of the final charge and didn't know you had paid another way.

Why blocking can be a problem

Blocking is used to make sure you don't exceed your credit line before checking out of a hotel or returning a rental car, leaving the merchant unpaid.

If you're nowhere near your credit limit, chances are that blocking won't be a problem. But if you're reaching the limit, be careful. Not only can it be embarrassing to have your card declined, but it also can be inconvenient, especially if you have an emergency purchase and no available credit.

How to avoid blocking

To avoid the aggravation that blocking can cause, follow these tips:

- ❑ Consider paying hotel, motel, or rental car bills with the same credit card you used at the beginning of the transaction.
- ❑ When you check into a hotel or rent a car, ask clerks how much will be blocked and how the amount is determined.
- ❑ If you pay with a different credit card or with cash or a check, ask the clerk to remove the block.

In addition, when you choose a credit card, ask issuers how long they block credit lines for transactions involving hotels, motels, and rental cars. You may want to go with an issuer that uses short blocks.

Lost or stolen credit and ATM cards

Many people find it easy and convenient to use credit and ATM cards. The Fair Credit Billing Act (FCBA) and the Electronic Fund Transfer Act (EFTA) offer procedures for you and businesses to use if your cards are lost or stolen.

Limiting your financial loss

Report the loss or theft of your credit and ATM cards to the card issuers as quickly as possible. Most companies have toll-free numbers and 24-hour service to deal with such emergencies. It's a good idea to follow up your phone calls with a letter that includes your account number, when you noticed your card was missing, and the date you first reported the loss.

You also may want to check your homeowner's insurance policy to see if it covers your liability for card thefts. If not, some insurance companies will allow you to change your policy to include this protection.

Credit card loss

If you report the loss before a card is used, you cannot be held responsible for any unauthorized charges. If a thief uses your card before you report it missing, the most you will owe for unauthorized charges is $50 per card. This is true even if a thief uses your credit card at an ATM machine to access your credit card account.

However, it's not enough simply to report your credit card loss. After the loss, review your billing statements carefully. If they show any unauthorized charges, send a letter to the card issuer describing each questionable charge. Again, tell the card issuer the date your card was lost or stolen and when you first reported it to them. Be sure to send the letter to the address provided for billing errors. Do not send it with a payment or to the address where you send your payments unless you are directed to do so.

ATM card loss

If you report an ATM card missing before it's used without your permission, the EFTA says the card issuer cannot hold you responsible for any unauthorized withdrawals. If unauthorized use occurs before you report it, the amount you can be held liable for depends upon how quickly you report the loss. For example, if you report the loss within two business days after you realize your card is missing, you will not be responsible for more than $50 for unauthorized use.

However, if you don't report the loss within two business days after you discover the loss, you could lose up to $500 because of an unauthorized withdrawal. You risk unlimited loss if you fail to report an unauthorized transfer or withdrawal within 60 days after your bank statement is mailed to you. That means you could lose all the money in your bank account and the unused portion of your line of credit established for overdrafts.

If unauthorized transactions show up on your bank statement, report them to the card issuer as quickly as possible. Once you've reported the loss of your ATM card, you cannot be held liable for additional amounts, even if more unauthorized transactions are made.

Protecting your cards

The best protections against card fraud are to know where your cards are at all times and to keep them secure. For ATM card protection, it's important to keep your Personal Identification Number (PIN) a secret. Don't use your address, birthdate, phone number, or Social Security number. Memorize your PIN. Statistics show that in one-third of ATM card frauds, cardholders wrote their PINS on their ATM cards or on slips of paper kept with their cards.

The following suggestions may help you protect your credit and ATM card accounts.

For credit cards:

- ❑ Be cautious about disclosing your account number over the phone unless you know you are dealing with a reputable company.
- ❑ Never put your account number on the outside of an envelope or on a postcard.
- ❑ Draw a line through blank spaces on charge slips above the total so the amount cannot be changed.
- ❑ Don't sign a blank charge slip.
- ❑ Tear up carbons and save your receipts to check against your monthly billing statements.
- ❑ Open billing statements promptly and compare them with your receipts. Report mistakes or discrepancies as soon as possible to the special address listed on your statement for "billing inquiries." Under the FCBA, the card issuer must investigate billing errors reported to them within 60 days of the date your statement was mailed to you.
- ❑ Keep a record—in a safe place separate from your cards—of your account numbers, expiration dates, and the telephone numbers of each card issuer so you can report a loss quickly.
- ❑ Carry only those cards that you anticipate you'll need.

For ATM cards:

- ❑ Don't carry your PIN in your wallet or purse or write it on your ATM card.
- ❑ Never write your PIN on the outside of a deposit slip or envelope or on a postcard.
- ❑ Take your ATM receipt after completing a transaction.
- ❑ Reconcile all ATM receipts with bank statements as soon as possible.

Buying a registration service

For an annual fee of $10 to $35, companies will notify the issuers of your credit and ATM accounts if your card is lost or stolen. This service allows you to make only one phone call to report all card losses rather than calling individual issuers. Most services also will request replacement cards on your behalf.

Purchasing a card registration service may be convenient, but it's not required. The FCBA and the EFTA give you the right to contact your card issuers directly in the event of a loss or suspected unauthorized use.

If you decide to buy a registration service, compare offers. Carefully read the contract to determine the company's obligations and your liability. For example, will the company reimburse you if it fails to notify card issuers promptly once you've called in the loss to the service? If not, you could be liable for unauthorized charges.

Credit card loss protection offers

"A man told me that the Y2K bug makes it easier for thieves to get my credit card number and charge thousands of dollars on my account. He said that I'd be responsible for paying the bills, even though I didn't okay the charges. He wanted to sell me credit card loss protection insurance to cover the unauthorized charges, and said that the fee for the insurance could be billed to my credit card. Should I buy it?"

❑ ❑ ❑

"I got a call from a woman who said I need credit card loss protection insurance. I thought there was a law that limited my liability to $50 for unauthorized charges. But she said the law had changed and that now, people are liable for all unauthorized charges on their account. Is that true?"

❑ ❑ ❑

Don't buy the pitch—and don't buy the "loss protection" insurance. Telephone scam artists are lying to get people to buy worthless credit card loss protection and insurance programs. If you didn't authorize a charge, don't pay it. Follow your credit card issuer's procedures for disputing charges you haven't authorized. According to the Federal Trade Commission, your liability for unauthorized charges is limited to $50.

The FTC says worthless credit card loss protection offers are becoming more common as fraudulent promoters try to exploit consumer uncertainty. As a result, the agency is cautioning consumers to avoid doing business with callers who claim that:

- ❑ You are liable for more than $50 in unauthorized charges on your credit card account.
- ❑ You need credit card loss protection because computer hackers can access your credit card number and charge thousands of dollars to your account.
- ❑ They are from "the security department" and want to activate the protection feature on your credit card.

The FTC advises consumers not to give out personal information—including their credit card or bank account numbers—over the phone or online for any product unless they are familiar with the business and have initiated the contact. Scam artists can use your personal information to commit fraud.

Gold and platinum cards

If you're looking for credit, be wary of some gold or platinum card offers promising to get you credit cards or improve your credit rating.

Although they claim to be general-purpose credit cards, some gold or platinum cards permit you to buy merchandise only from specialized catalogues. Marketers of these credit cards often promise that by participating in their credit programs, you will be able to get major credit cards (such as an unsecured Visa or MasterCard), lines of credit from national specialty and department stores, better credit reports, and other financial benefits.

Rarely, however, can you improve your credit rating or get major credit cards by buying gold or platinum credit cards. Often the only major credit card you might get is a secured credit card that requires a substantial security deposit with a bank. In addition, many of these credit card offerors do not report to credit bureaus as they promise, and their cards seldom help secure lines of credit with other creditors.

Gold and platinum credit card offers are usually promoted through television or newspaper advertisements, direct mail, or telephone solicitations using automatic dialing machines and recorded messages. People who live in lower-income areas often are the target of these sales pitches.

Be wary of gold and platinum card promotions that:

- ❑ Charge upfront fees without saying there may be additional costs. Some gold or platinum card promoters charge $50 or more for their cards. Only after you agree to pay this fee are you told there's an additional fee, sometimes $30 or more, to get the merchandise catalogues. Yet these catalogues are the only places you can use the cards.
- ❑ Use 900 or 976 telephone exchanges. You pay for phone calls with these prefixes—even if you never get the gold or platinum card. The cost for these calls can be high.
- ❑ Misrepresent prices and payments for merchandise. You're not allowed to charge the total amount when you buy merchandise from gold or platinum card catalogues. Instead, you often must pay a cash deposit on each item you charge—an amount usually equal to what the company paid for the product. Only after you pay your deposit can you charge the balance. Also, catalogue prices can be much higher than discount store prices.
- ❑ Promise to easily get you better credit. Marketers of these cards often claim it's easy to get major credit cards after using their cards for a few months. In fact, the

only major cards you usually can get through these marketers are secured. A secured card requires you to open and maintain a savings account as security for your line of credit. The required deposit may range from a few hundred to several thousand dollars. Your credit line is a percentage of the deposit, typically 50 to 100 percent.

How to protect yourself

Follow these precautions to avoid becoming a victim of gold and platinum card scams:

- ❑ Think twice about any offer to get "easy credit."
- ❑ Be skeptical of promises to erase bad credit or to secure major credit cards regardless of your past credit problems. There are no "easy" solutions to a poor credit rating that's based on accurate information. Only time and good credit habits will restore your credit worthiness.
- ❑ Investigate an offer before enrolling.
- ❑ Contact your local Better Business Bureau, consumer protection agency, or state attorney general's office to see if any complaints have been filed against a particular promoter of gold or platinum cards.
- ❑ If a marketer promises that a card is accepted at certain retail chains, verify it with the stores.
- ❑ If a marketer assures you that reliable information about you will be reported to credit bureaus, call the bureaus to confirm that the merchant is a member. Unless gold or platinum card merchants are subscribers to credit bureaus, they won't be able to report information about your credit experience.
- ❑ Be cautious about calling 900 or 976 telephone numbers. Calls to numbers with 900 or 976 prefixes cost money. Don't confuse these exchanges with toll-free 800 numbers. If you dial a pay-per-call number mistakenly,

contact your local phone company immediately. They may be able to remove the charge from your bill.

Secured credit card marketing scams

ANYONE CAN QUALIFY FOR A MAJOR CREDIT CARD!
Separated? Divorced? Bankrupt? Widowed?
BAD CREDIT? NO CREDIT? NO PROBLEM!
900-555-1111
* Make the call NOW and get the credit you deserve!
* Even if you've been turned down before,
you owe it to yourself and your family.
* Your major credit card is waiting.

❑ ❑ ❑

Ads like this one may appeal to you if you have a poor credit history or no credit at all. Although secured credit cards can be an effective way to build or reestablish your credit history, some marketers of secured cards make deceptive advertising claims to entice you to respond to their ads.

Secured vs. unsecured cards

Secured and unsecured cards can be used to pay for goods and services. However, a secured card requires you to open and maintain a savings account as security for your line of credit; an unsecured card does not.

The required savings deposit for a secured card may range from a few hundred to several thousand dollars. Your credit line is a percentage of your deposit, typically 50 to 100 percent. Usually, a bank will pay interest on your deposit. In addition, you also may have to pay application and processing fees—sometimes totaling hundreds of dollars. Before you apply, be sure to ask what the total fees are and whether they will be refunded if you're denied a card. Typically, a secured card requires an annual fee and has a higher interest rate than an unsecured card.

Deceptive ads and scams

The Federal Trade Commission (FTC) has taken action against companies that deceptively advertise major credit cards through television, newspapers, and postcards. The ads may offer unsecured credit cards or secured credit cards, or they may not specify a card type. The ads usually lead you to believe you can get a card simply by calling the number listed. Sometimes the number is not toll-free. A 900 number service, for which you are billed just for making the call, may instruct you to give your name and address to receive a credit application, or give you a list of banks offering secured cards. It also may tell you to call another 900 number (at an additional charge) for more information.

Deceptive ads often leave out important information, such as:

- ❑ The cost of the 900 call, which can range from \$2 to \$50 or more.
- ❑ The required security deposit, application, and processing fees.
- ❑ Eligibility requirements, such as income or age.
- ❑ An annual fee or the fact that the secured card has a higher-than-average interest rate on any balance.

How to avoid the scam

To avoid being victimized, look for the following signs:

- ❑ Offers of easy credit. No one can guarantee to get you credit. Before deciding whether to give you a credit card, legitimate credit providers examine your credit report.
- ❑ A call to a 900 number for a credit card. You pay for calls with a 900 prefix, whether you receive a credit card or not.
- ❑ Credit cards offered by "credit repair" companies or "credit clinics." These businesses also may offer to clean up your credit history for a fee. However, you can correct genuine mistakes or outdated information yourself

by contacting credit bureaus directly. Remember that only time and good credit habits will restore your credit worthiness.

Credit reporting

If you're considering a secured card as a way to build or reestablish a credit record, make sure the issuer reports to a credit bureau. Your credit history is maintained by companies called credit bureaus; they collect information reported to them by banks, mortgage companies, department stores, and other creditors. If your card issuer doesn't report to a bureau, the card won't help you build a credit history.

For more information

To build a credit record, you may want to apply for a charge card or a small loan at a local store or lending institution. Ask if the creditor reports transactions to a credit bureau. If they do—and if you pay back your debts regularly—you will build a good credit history.

If you cannot get credit on your own, ask a relative or friend with a good credit history to act as your cosigner. The cosigner promises to repay the debt if you don't.

If you're interested in applying for a secured credit card, the BankCard Holders of America (BHA) provides a list of institutions offering secured cards. Send a check or money order for $4 to:

Secured Credit Card List
BHA Customer Service
524 Branch Drive
Salem, VA 24153

Chapter 9

Lending Scams

Advance-fee loan scams

Sometimes the way out of debt may seem to be more debt. If you're thinking of taking out a loan to repay debt, beware of advertisements for "advance-fee" or "guaranteed" loans. The FTC investigates complaints about companies that guarantee loans for financially strapped consumers and small business owners.

Advertisements that promise loans generally appear in the classified sections of local and national newspapers, magazines, and tabloids. They also may appear in mailings, in radio spots, and on local cable channels. Often, 900 numbers that result in charges on your phone bill or toll-free 800 numbers are featured in the ads. These companies also prefer to use delivery systems other than the U.S. Postal Service, such as overnight or courier services, to avoid detection and prosecution by postal authorities.

Some companies claim they can guarantee you a loan for a fee paid in advance. The fee may range from $100 to several hundred dollars. Small businesses have been charged as much as several thousand dollars as an advance fee for a loan.

Legitimate credit grantors may charge fees to process your loan application, but they will not guarantee that you will qualify for a loan. Illicit advance-fee loan schemes, on the other hand, either promise or strongly suggest that a loan will be provided in exchange for an up-front fee. Salespeople for such companies also may verbally promise that some or all of your advance fee will be refunded if your application is unsuccessful. Some fraudulent companies also may claim that your advance fee will be credited toward repayment of the loan. Usually none of these claims is true.

The FTC suggests taking the following precautions before responding to ads for advance-fee loans:

Be wary of advertising claiming bad credit is not a problem in securing a loan. If money is not available to you through traditional lending institutions, it is unlikely to become available in response to a classified ad.

Be cautious of lenders who use 900 numbers. You may call a toll-free number that then directs you to dial a 900 number. You pay for 900-number calls, of course, and the charges may be high.

Check out the company. Contact your local consumer protection agency and the state attorney general's office to learn if they have received any complaints about companies offering advance-fee loans. Keep in mind, however, that suspect companies often establish their operations in one state, advertise heavily for only a few months, and collect their loan fees, only to close up shop and move on to another state before complaints are registered and local authorities have a chance to act. Therefore, just because your local consumer protection agency has no complaints on file does not mean that an advance-fee loan business is legitimate.

Be careful about making any loan agreements over the telephone. Do not give your credit card, checking account, or Social Security numbers over the phone unless you are familiar with the company. This information can be used against you with other frauds. For example, if you give your checking account number over the phone to a stranger for "verification" or "computer purposes," the number may be used to debit (withdraw) money from your checking account.

Ask to review any company's offer in writing. Also, make sure you understand the terms of the agreement before you complete the transaction.

Obviously there are plenty of pitfalls in the credit repair business. Recent federal legislation has attempted to deal with fraudulent practices, but it remains to be seen if the new statutes will be effective in stopping the scam artists. One important loophole in the law is that nonprofit organizations are exempt from its requirements, and experience in California has shown that repair companies will apply for tax-exempt status, some by offering senior discounts or consumer education to qualify. In California, other companies either ignored the law or went underground with their services by incorporating credit consulting into another type of business such as real estate, financial planning or auto brokering.

Acquaint yourself with the law, and you'll be prepared if and when a scam artist strikes. For a summary of laws affecting consumer credit information and repair services, see Appendix A.

Home equity scams

Do you own your home? If so, it's likely to be your greatest single asset. Unfortunately, if you agree to a loan that's based on the equity you have in your home, you may be putting your most valuable asset at risk.

Homeowners—particularly those who are elderly, minorities, and with low incomes or poor credit—should be careful when borrowing money based on their home equity. Why? Certain abusive or exploitative lenders target these borrowers, who unwittingly may be putting their homes on the line.

Abusive lending practices range from equity stripping and loan flipping to hiding loan terms and packing a loan with extra charges. The Federal Trade Commission urges you to be aware of these loan practices to avoid losing your home.

The practices

Equity stripping

You need money. You don't have much income coming in each month. You have built up equity in your home. A lender tells you that you can get a loan, even though you know your income is just not enough to keep up with the monthly payments. The lender encourages you to "pad" your income on your application form to help get the loan approved.

This lender may be out to steal the equity you have built up in your home. The lender doesn't care if you can't keep up with the monthly payments. As soon as you don't, the lender will foreclose, taking your home and stripping you of the equity you have spent years building. If you take out a loan but don't have enough income to make the monthly payments, you are being set up. You will probably lose your home.

The balloon payment

You've fallen behind in your mortgage payments and may face foreclosure. Another lender offers to save you from foreclosure by refinancing your mortgage and lowering your monthly payments. Look carefully at the loan terms. The payments may be lower because the lender is offering a loan on which you repay only the interest each month. At the end of the loan term, the principal (that is, the entire amount that you borrowed) is due in one lump sum called a balloon payment. If you can't make the balloon payment or refinance, you face foreclosure and the loss of your home.

Loan flipping

Suppose you've had your mortgage for years. The interest rate is low and the monthly payments fit nicely into your budget, but you could use some extra money. A lender calls to talk about refinancing and, using the availability of extra cash as bait, claims it's time the equity in your home started "working" for you. You agree to refinance your loan. After you've made a few payments on the loan, the lender calls to offer you a bigger loan for, say, a vacation. If you accept the offer, the lender refinances your original loan and then lends you additional money. In this practice (often called "flipping") the lender charges you high points and fees each time you refinance, and may increase your interest rate as well. If the loan has a prepayment penalty, you will have to pay that penalty each time you take out a new loan.

You now have some extra money and a lot more debt, stretched out over a longer time. The extra cash you receive may be less than the additional costs and fees you were charged for the refinancing. And what's worse, you are now paying interest on those extra fees charged in each refinancing. Long story short? With each refinancing, you've increased your debt and are probably paying a very high price for some extra cash. After a while, if you get in over your head and can't pay, you could lose your home.

The "home improvement" loan

A contractor calls or knocks on your door and offers to install a new roof or remodel your kitchen at a price that sounds reasonable. You tell him you're interested but can't afford it. He tells you that he can arrange financing through a lender he knows. You agree to the project, and the contractor begins work. At some point after the contractor begins, you are asked to sign a lot of papers. The papers may be blank or the lender may rush you to sign before you have time to read what you've been given. The contractor threatens to leave the work on your house unfinished if you don't sign, so you sign the papers. Only later do you realize that the papers you signed are a home equity loan. The interest rate, points, and fees seem very high. To make matters worse, the work on your home isn't done right or hasn't been completed, and the contractor, who may have been paid by the lender, has little interest in completing the work to your satisfaction.

Credit insurance packing

You've just agreed to a mortgage on terms you think you can afford. At closing, the lender gives you papers to sign that include charges for credit insurance or other "benefits" that you did not ask for and do not want. The lender hopes you don't notice this, and that you just sign the loan papers where you are asked to sign. The lender doesn't explain exactly how much extra money this will cost you each month on your loan. If you do notice, you're afraid that if you ask questions or object, you might not get the loan. The lender may tell you that this insurance comes with the loan, making you think that it comes at no additional cost. Or, if you object, the lender may even tell you that if you want the loan without the insurance, the loan papers will have to be rewritten, that it could take several days, and that the manager may reconsider the loan altogether. If you agree to buy the insurance, you really are paying extra for the loan by buying a product you may not want or need.

Mortgage servicing abuses

After you get a mortgage, you receive a letter from your lender saying that your monthly payments will be higher than you expected. The lender says that your payments include escrow for taxes and insurance, even though you arranged to pay those items yourself with the lender's okay. Later, a message from the lender says you are being charged late fees. But you know your payments were on time. Or, you may receive a message saying that you failed to maintain required property insurance and the lender is buying more costly insurance at your expense. Other charges that you don't understand, such as legal fees, are added to the amount you owe, increasing your monthly payments or the amount you owe at the end of the loan term. The lender doesn't provide you with an accurate or complete account of these charges. You ask for a payoff statement to refinance with another lender and receive a statement that's inaccurate or incomplete. The lender's actions make it almost impossible to determine how much you've paid or how much you owe. You may pay more than you owe.

Signing over your deed

If you're having trouble paying your mortgage and the lender has threatened to foreclose and take your home, you may feel desperate.

Another "lender" may contact you with an offer to help you find new financing. Before he can help you, he asks you to deed your property to him, claiming that it's a temporary measure to prevent foreclosure. The promised refinancing that would let you save your home never comes through.

Once the lender has the deed to your property, he starts to treat it as his own. He may borrow against it (for his benefit, not yours) or even sell it to someone else. Because you don't own the home any more, you won't get any money when the property is sold. The lender will treat you as a tenant and your mortgage payments as rent. If your "rent" payments are late, you can be evicted from your home.

Protecting yourself

You can protect yourself against losing your home to inappropriate lending practices. Here's how:

Don't:

- ❏ Agree to a home equity loan if you don't have enough income to make the monthly payments.
- ❏ Sign any document you haven't read or any document that has blank spaces to be filled in after you sign.
- ❏ Let anyone pressure you into signing any document.
- ❏ Agree to a loan that includes credit insurance or extra products you don't want.
- ❏ Let the promise of extra cash or lower monthly payments get in the way of your good judgment about whether the cost you will pay for the loan is really worth it.
- ❏ Deed your property to anyone.

Do:

- ❏ Ask specifically if credit insurance is required as a condition of the loan. If it isn't, and a charge is included in your loan and you don't want the insurance, ask that the charge be removed from the loan documents. If you want the added security of credit insurance, shop around for the best rates.

- ❑ Keep careful records of what you've paid, including billing statements and canceled checks. Challenge any charge you think is inaccurate.
- ❑ Check contractors' references when it is time to have work done in your home. Get more than one estimate.
- ❑ Read all items carefully. If you need an explanation of any terms or conditions, talk to someone you can trust, such as a knowledgeable family member or an attorney. Consider all the costs of financing before you agree to a loan.

Auto and home loans

Debt repayment plans usually cover unsecured debt. Your auto and home loans, which are considered secured debt, may not be included. You must continue to make payments to these creditors directly.

Most automobile financing agreements allow a creditor to repossess your car any time you're in default. No notice is required. If your car is repossessed, you may have to pay the full balance due on the loan, as well as towing and storage costs, to get it back. If you can't do this, the creditor may sell the car. If you see default approaching, you may be better off selling the car yourself and paying off the debt. This way, you would avoid the added costs of repossession and a negative entry on your credit report.

If you fall behind on your mortgage, contact your lender immediately to avoid foreclosure. Most lenders are willing to work with you if they believe you're acting in good faith and if the situation is temporary. Some lenders may reduce or suspend your payments for a short time. When you resume regular payments, though, you may have to pay an additional amount toward the past due total. Other lenders may agree to change the terms of the mortgage by extending the repayment period to reduce the monthly debt. Ask whether additional fees would be assessed for these changes, and calculate how much they total in the long run.

If you and your lender cannot work out a plan, contact a housing counseling agency. Some agencies limit their counseling service to homeowners with FHA mortgages, but many offer free help to any homeowner who's having trouble making mortgage payments. Call the local office of the Department of Housing and Urban Development (HUD) or the housing authority in your state, city, or county for help in finding a housing counseling agency near you.

Debt consolidation

You may be able to lower your cost of credit by consolidating your debt through a second mortgage or a home equity line of credit. Think carefully before taking this on. These loans require your home as collateral. If you can't make the payments or if the payments are late, you could lose your home.

The costs of these consolidation loans can add up. In addition to interest on the loan, you pay "points." Typically, one point is equal to 1 percent of the amount you borrow. Still, these loans may provide certain tax advantages that are not available with other kinds of credit.

Payday loans

- ❑ "I just need enough cash to tide me over until payday."
- ❑ "GET CASH UNTIL PAYDAY!...$100 OR MORE...FAST."

These kinds of ads are on the radio, television, the Internet, and even in the mail. They refer to payday loans, which come at a very high price.

Check cashers, finance companies, and others are making small, short-term, high-rate loans that go by a variety of names: payday loans, cash advance loans, check advance loans, post-dated check loans, or deferred deposit check loans.

Usually, a borrower writes a personal check (payable to the lender) for the amount he or she wishes to borrow plus a fee. The company gives the borrower the amount of the check minus the fee. Fees charged for payday loans are usually a percentage of the face value of the check or a fee charged per amount borrowed. If you extend or "roll over" the loan, say for another two weeks, you will pay the fees for each extension.

Under the Truth in Lending Act, the cost of payday loans (as with other types of credit) must be disclosed. Among other information, you must receive, in writing, the finance charge (a dollar amount) and the annual percentage rate (the cost of credit on a yearly basis).

A cash advance loan secured by a personal check, such as a payday loan, is very expensive credit. Let's say you write a personal check for $115 to borrow $100 for up to 14 days. The check casher or payday lender agrees to hold the check until your next payday. At that time, depending on the particular plan, the lender deposits the check, you redeem the check by paying the $115 in cash, or you pay a fee to extend the loan for another two weeks. In this example, the cost of the initial loan is a $15 finance charge and 390 percent APR. If you roll over the loan three times, the finance charge would climb to $60 to borrow $100.

Alternatives to payday loans

There are other options. Consider the possibilities before choosing a payday loan:

- ❑ When you need credit, shop carefully. Compare offers. Look for the credit offer with the lowest APR. Consider a small loan from your credit union or small loan company, an advance on pay from your employer, or a loan from family or friends. A cash advance on a credit card also may be a possibility, but it may have a higher interest rate than your other sources of funds. Find out the terms before you decide. Also, a local community-based organization may make small business loans to individuals.

- ❑ Compare the APR and the finance charge (which includes loan fees, interest, and other types of credit costs) of credit offers to get the lowest cost.
- ❑ Ask your creditors for more time to pay your bills. Find out what they will charge for that service—as a late charge, an additional finance charge, or a higher interest rate.
- ❑ Make a realistic budget, and figure your monthly and daily expenditures. Avoid unnecessary purchases—even small daily items. Their costs add up. Also, build some savings (even if it's a small amount) to avoid borrowing for emergencies, unexpected expenses, or other items. For example, by putting the amount of the fee that would be paid on a typical $300 payday loan in a savings account for six months, you would have extra money available. This can give you a buffer against financial emergencies.
- ❑ Find out if you have, or can get, overdraft protection on your checking account. If you are regularly using most or all of the funds in your account and if you make a mistake in your checking (or savings) account ledger or records, overdraft protection can help protect you from further credit problems. Find out the terms of overdraft protection.
- ❑ If you need help working out a debt repayment plan with creditors or developing a budget, contact your local consumer credit counseling service. There are nonprofit groups in every state that offer credit guidance to consumers. These services are available at little or no cost. Also check with your employer, credit union, or housing authority for no- or low-cost credit counseling programs.
- ❑ If you decide you must use a payday loan, borrow only as much as you can afford to pay with your next paycheck and still have enough to make it to the next payday.

Chapter 10

Dealing with Debt

Are you having trouble paying your bills? Are you getting cancellation notices from creditors? Are your accounts being turned over to debt collectors? Are you worried about losing your home or your car? If you answered yes to any (or all) of these questions, you're not alone. Many people face financial crises at some time in their lives. Whether the crisis is caused by personal or family illness, the loss of a job, or simple overspending, it can seem overwhelming, but often it can be overcome. The fact of the matter is that your financial situation doesn't have to go from bad to worse.

If you or someone you know is in financial hot water, consider these options: realistic budgeting, credit counseling from a reputable organization, debt consolidation, or bankruptcy. How do you know which will work best for you? It depends on your level of debt, your level of discipline, and your prospects for the future.

Developing a budget

The first step toward taking control of your financial situation is to take a realistic assessment of how much money comes in and how much money you spend. Start by listing your income from all sources. Then list your "fixed" expenses (those that are the same each month, such as your mortgage or rent payment, car payment, and insurance premiums). Next, list the expenses that vary, such as entertainment, recreation, and clothing. Writing down all your expenses—

even those that seem insignificant, such as a cup of coffee on your way to work—is a helpful way to track your spending patterns, identify the expenses that are necessary, and prioritize the rest. The goal is to make sure you can make ends meet on the basics: housing, food, healthcare, insurance, and education.

Your public library has information about budgeting and money management techniques. Low-cost budget counseling services that can help you analyze your income and expenses and develop a budget and spending plan also are available in most communities. Check your telephone book or contact your local bank or consumer protection office for information about them. In addition, many universities, military bases, credit unions, and housing authorities operate nonprofit financial counseling programs.

Contacting your creditors

Contact your creditors immediately if you are having trouble making ends meet. Tell them why it's difficult for you, and try to work out a modified payment plan that reduces your payments to a more manageable level. Don't wait until your accounts have been turned over to a debt collector. At that point, the creditors have given up on you.

Dealing with debt collectors

The Fair Debt Collection Practices Act is the federal law that dictates how and when a debt collector may contact you. A debt collector may not call you before 8 a.m., after 9 p.m., or at work if the collector knows that your employer doesn't approve of the calls. Collectors may not harass you, make false statements, or use unfair practices when they try to collect a debt. Debt collectors must honor a written request from you to stop further contact.

Credit counseling

If you aren't disciplined enough to create a workable budget and stick to it, can't work out a repayment plan with your creditors, or can't keep track of mounting bills, consider contacting a credit counseling service. Your creditors may be willing to accept reduced payments if you enter into a debt repayment plan with a reputable organization. In these plans, you deposit money each month with the credit counseling service. Your deposits are used to pay your creditors according to a payment schedule developed by the counselor. As part of the repayment plan, you may have to agree not to apply for—or use—any additional credit while you're participating in the program.

A successful repayment plan requires you to make regular, timely payments, and could take 48 months or longer to complete. Ask the credit counseling service for an estimate of the time it will take you to complete the plan. Some services charge little or nothing for managing the plan; others charge a monthly fee that could add up to a significant amount over time. Some credit counseling services are funded, in part, by contributions from creditors.

Although a debt repayment plan can eliminate much of the stress that comes from dealing with creditors and overdue bills, it does not mean you can forget about your debts. You still are responsible for paying any creditors whose debts are not included in the plan. You are responsible for reviewing monthly statements from your creditors to make sure your payments have been received. If your repayment plan depends on your creditors agreeing to lower or eliminate interest and finance charges, or waive late fees, you are responsible for making sure these concessions are reflected on your statements.

A debt repayment plan does not erase your negative credit history. Accurate information about your accounts can stay on your credit report for up to seven years. In addition, your creditors will continue to report information about accounts that are handled through a debt repayment plan. For example, creditors may report that an account is in financial counseling, that payments have been late or missed altogether, or that there are write-offs or other concessions. A demonstrated pattern of timely payments, however, will help you get credit in the future.

Bankruptcy

Personal bankruptcy generally is considered the debt management tool of last resort because the results are long-lasting and far-reaching. A bankruptcy stays on your credit report for 10 years, making it difficult to acquire credit, buy a home, get life insurance, or sometimes get a job. However, it is a legal procedure that offers a fresh start for people who can't satisfy their debts. Individuals who follow the bankruptcy rules receive a discharge (a court order that says they do not have to repay certain debts).

There are two primary types of personal bankruptcy: Chapter 13 and Chapter 7. Each must be filed in federal bankruptcy court. The current fees for seeking bankruptcy relief are $160 (a $130 filing fee and a $30 administrative fee). Attorney fees are additional and can vary widely. The consequences of bankruptcy are significant and require careful consideration.

Chapter 13 allows you, if you have a regular income and limited debt, to keep property, such as a mortgaged house or car, that you otherwise might lose. The court approves a repayment plan that allows you to pay off a default during a period of three to five years, rather than surrender any property.

Chapter 7, known as straight bankruptcy, involves liquidating all assets that are not exempt. Exempt property may include cars, work-related tools, and basic household furnishings. Some property may be sold by a court-appointed official (a trustee) or turned over to creditors. You can receive a discharge of your debts under Chapter 7 only once every six years.

Both types of bankruptcy may get rid of unsecured debts and stop foreclosures, repossessions, garnishments, utility shut-offs, and debt collection activities. Both also provide exemptions that allow you to keep certain assets, although exemption amounts vary. Personal bankruptcy usually does not erase child support, alimony, fines, taxes, and some student loan obligations. Also, unless you have an acceptable plan to catch up on your debt under Chapter 13, bankruptcy usually does not allow you to keep property when your creditor has an unpaid mortgage or lien on it.

Debt relief–promising advertisements

Consumer debt is at an all-time high. What's more, record numbers of consumers—more than 1 million in the year 2000—are filing for bankruptcy. Whether your debt dilemma is the result of an illness, unemployment, or overspending, it can seem overwhelming. In your effort to get solvent, be on the alert for advertisements that offer seemingly quick fixes. The ads pitch the promise of debt relief, but they rarely say relief may be spelled b-a-n-k-r-u-p-t-c-y. And although bankruptcy is one option to deal with financial problems, it's generally considered the option of last resort because of its long-term negative impact on your creditworthiness. A bankruptcy stays on your credit report for 10 years, and it can hinder your ability to get credit, a job, insurance, or even a place to live.

The Federal Trade Commission cautions consumers to read between the lines when faced with ads in newspapers, magazines or even telephone directories that say:

- "Consolidate your bills into one monthly payment without borrowing."
- "STOP credit harassment, foreclosures, repossessions, tax levies and garnishments."
- "Keep Your Property."
- "Wipe out your debts! Consolidate your bills! How? By using the protection and assistance provided by federal law. For once, let the law work for you!"

Such phrases often involve bankruptcy proceedings, which can hurt your credit and cost you attorneys' fees.

If you're having trouble paying your bills, consider these possibilities before considering filing for bankruptcy:

- Talk with your creditors. They may be willing to work out a modified payment plan.

- ❑ Contact a credit counseling service. These organizations work with you and your creditors to develop debt repayment plans. Such plans require you to deposit money each month with the counseling service. The service then pays your creditors. Some nonprofit organizations charge little or nothing for their services.
- ❑ Carefully consider a second mortgage or home equity line of credit. Although these loans may allow you to consolidate your debt, they also require your home as collateral.

Finding low-cost help for credit problems

It's a good idea to try to solve your debt problems with your creditors as soon as you realize you won't be able to make your payments. If you can't resolve your credit problems yourself or need additional help, you may want to contact a credit counseling service. There are nonprofit organizations in every state that counsel and educate individuals and families on debt problems, budgeting, and using credit wisely. These organizations work directly with your creditors to help resolve your debt problems by negotiating a repayment schedule that is affordable for you and acceptable to the creditor. There is little or no cost for these services.

Universities, military bases, credit unions, and housing authorities also may offer low- or no-cost credit counseling programs. Check the white pages of your telephone directory for a service near you.

For more information

To learn about your rights under the Telemarketing Sales Rule and how to protect yourself from fraudulent telephone sales practices, request a free copy of *Straight Talk About Telemarketing.* Contact: Consumer Response Center, Federal Trade Commission, 600 Pennsylvania Avenue, NW, Washington, D.C. 20580; toll free, at (877) FTC-HELP (877-382-4357); TDD 202-326-2502. You can also request a copy online at *www.ftc.gov.*

The following organizations have additional information:

American Financial Services Association
Education Foundation
919 Eighteenth Street, NW
Washington, D.C. 20006
www.afsaef.org

National Association of Consumer Agency Administrators
1010 Vermont Avenue, NW, Suite 514
Washington, D.C. 20005
www.nacaanet.org

Navy Personnel Command
Personnel and Family Readiness (PERS-662C3)
5720 Integrity Drive, Building 768
Millington, TN 38055-6620
www.mwr.navy.mil

Chapter 11

Credit Repair: Who needs it? What's wrong with it?

Who needs credit repair? If you're like 70 percent of credit-using consumers, the answer could well be you. You may have encountered past financial difficulties that affect your ability to use credit today. At some point in your life, you may develop a negative credit history that you need to overcome. Or you may be among the many unfortunate consumers with incorrect and negative information on your report. Although the credit reporting industry purports to be concerned with accuracy of information, errors are not uncommon, and trying to fix them can be an ordeal.

For instance, a woman in Santa Ana, Calif. wrote letters and made telephone calls to the major bureaus for six months in an attempt to get another person's bad credit history out of her file. A Chicago man with the same problem couldn't convince a credit bureau there was a mistake, even though the age and addresses of the similarly named man whose information appeared on his report were obviously different from his. A suburban St. Louis couple had a bankruptcy filing mistakenly placed in their file. Banks shut off loans to their struggling construction business, forcing them to file bankruptcy for real. They sued, but lost.

There's also the case of a Los Angeles woman whose credit was destroyed when someone used her Social Security number to open 15 fraudulent charge accounts and charged nearly $15,000 worth of merchandise. The woman challenged the credit bureau reports and informed them that information supplied on the credit applications—including name, birthdate, and employment—was incorrect, but the credit bureau did little to investigate her claim. She endured a two-and-a-half year credit nightmare, and in 1996, a federal jury awarded her $200,000 in damages when she sued Trans Union. She settled with Equifax and TRW (now Experian). The jury found that Trans Union had not conducted a investigation of her complaint or followed reasonable procedures to assure accuracy. It is required to do both by the Fair Credit Reporting Act (FCRA).

The credit bureau mentality

In their well-intentioned efforts to protect the integrity of the information they report, the major credit reporting bureaus have developed a mindset that, at times, seems determined to block, squelch, and otherwise frustrate consumers who are affected by the information they sell.

The bureaus try to report the truth about consumers and their spending/payment habits. Certainly there are deadbeats who want to fraudulently change accurate and negative information in their reports. At times, though, the bureaus are so vigilant in protecting reported information, it seems they are determined to prevent consumers from taking action to protect themselves and their credit reputations. Strategies for this include interpreting the FCRA in ways that support credit bureau inaction (hiding behind the law) and training subscribers to interpret neutral data in a negative way (too many inquiries make consumers a poor credit risk).

Industry secrecy

In determining whether to grant or deny credit, credit grantors use the five "C's": character, capacity, capital, collateral, and conditions. The major credit bureaus have developed an elaborate system by which to identify the "character" of a consumer. The system looks at the individual's credit report and, more specifically, his or her bill-paying habits.

Trade secrets and proprietary information are safeguarded and released only to those who have a "need" to know. For that reason, it is nearly impossible to find one individual within a credit bureau who is aware of all aspects of credit reporting. Credit bureaus have compartmentalized each of their operational and marketing functions so that individual employees know only one small aspect of the business.

Moreover, specific structures of power and influence within each department further promote this environment of secrecy. The public affairs and legislative affairs departments are used to convey information to the public and legislative and enforcement bodies. No matter how well-intentioned the managers of either of these departments may be, they simply parrot information that has been carefully guided through the corporate political maze.

Taking cover under the law

Congress enacted the Fair Credit Reporting Act as a means of protecting consumer rights. It was not intended to give specific authority for credit bureaus to operate a profit-making enterprise. However, the FCRA is precisely what credit bureaus quote most often in an attempt to legitimize questioned actions. For instance, Section 609 states, "Every consumer reporting agency shall, upon request and proper identification of any consumer, clearly and accurately disclose to the consumer...the recipients of any consumer report on the consumer which it has furnished for (A) employment purposes within the two-year period preceding the request, and (B) for any other purpose within the six-month period preceding the request."

The inquiry process is the means by which credit bureaus choose to conform to the above section. By policy, the inquiry remains on the file for a period of two years. Through workshops and publications, credit bureaus have taught their customers (subscribers) to view too many inquiries as a danger sign. As a result, having more than two inquiries is often cause for application rejection on a point score system.

In the recent past, a rash of consumer complaints occurred when consumers charged that no specific authorization was given to generate an inquiry into their credit records; however, credit bureaus in most cases declined to remove the inquiries through the dispute process as described in Section 611 of the FCRA. Moreover, consumers who complained to the credit bureaus received form letters indicating that their disputes would not be investigated.

An investigation by the Consumer Credit Commission showed that many of these consumers applied for a credit card with a major oil company, which generated an inquiry. The same oil company later generated a series of four additional inquiries to prevent the subsequent issuance of credit cards by competitors. Consumers who complained to the credit bureau were informed that inquiries must remain in their files for two years by law and that nothing could be done to eliminate this requirement.

What reports may *not* contain

Section 605 of the FCRA states: No consumer reporting agency may make any consumer report containing any of the following items of information:

- ❑ Cases under Title 11 of the United States Code or under the Bankruptcy Act that, from the date of entry of the order for relief or the date of adjudication, as the case may be, antedate the report by more than 20 years.
- ❑ Suits and judgments which, from date of entry, antedate the report by more than seven years or until the governing statute of limitations has expired, whichever is the longer period.
- ❑ Paid tax liens which, from date of payment, antedate the report by more than seven years.

- ❑ Accounts placed for collection or charged to profit and loss which antedate the report by more than seven years.
- ❑ Records of arrest, indictment, or conviction of crime which, from date of disposition, release, or parole, antedate the report by more than seven years.
- ❑ Any other adverse item of information which antedates the report by more than seven years.

Specifically, the law requires that "no" report shall be made containing any of the foregoing; however, credit bureaus repeatedly state to consumers that, according to the FCRA, negative information "must" be reported for seven years or, if it is bankruptcy related, 10 years.

Accuracy of information

Section 611 of the FCRA states: If the completeness or accuracy of any item of information contained in his file is disputed by the consumer, and such dispute is directly conveyed to the consumer reporting agency by the consumer, the consumer reporting agency shall, within a reasonable period of time, reinvestigate and record the current status of that information unless it has reasonable grounds to believe that the dispute by the consumer is frivolous or irrelevant. If after such reinvestigation such information is found to be inaccurate or can no longer be verified, the consumer reporting agency shall promptly delete such information.

In recent years, TRW (now Experian) generated thousands of form letters and sent them to consumers who disputed information from their credit files. The letter informed these consumers that their disputes were determined to be "frivolous and irrelevant" and thus would not be reinvestigated.

The phrase "frivolous and irrelevant" is somewhat ambiguous and needs appropriate clarification. Certainly, the wording of a dispute could lead a credit bureau to believe it is frivolous and irrelevant. For instance, such a dispute might read, "I was 60 days delinquent in making a payment because I was in the hospital and could not make the payments." Although this statement may be true and indeed unfortunate, the bureau considers it frivolous and irrelevant because it merely confirms the information on the report and does not challenge fact.

According to the Federal Trade Commission, disputes that call for action should not be considered frivolous and irrelevant. An example might be, "I was never late in making my payments; you have me confused with someone else. Please reinvestigate this matter."

Credit bureaus claim the majority of disputes received are deceptive. The legal "test" falls under the heading of "good faith belief." Good faith belief is determined through the use of the consumer's good memory and substantiating records.

❑ ❑ ❑

Nation's Big Three Consumer Reporting Agencies Agree To Pay $2.5 Million To Settle FTC Charges of Violating Fair Credit Reporting Act

On January 13, 2000 the Big Three national consumer reporting agencies, Equifax Credit Information Services, Inc., (Equifax), Trans Union LLC (Trans Union), and Experian Information Solutions, Inc. (Experian), agreed to a total of $2.5 million in payments as part of settlements negotiated by the Federal Trade Commission to resolve charges that they each violated provisions of the Fair Credit Reporting Act (FCRA) by failing to maintain a toll-free telephone number at which personnel are accessible to consumers during normal business hours. According to the FTC's complaints, Equifax, Trans Union, and Experian (collectively, consumer reporting agencies or CRAs) blocked millions of calls from consumers who wanted to discuss the contents and possible errors in their credit reports and kept some of those consumers on hold for unreasonably long periods of time. The proposed settlements with each CRA also would require that it meet specific performance standards to ensure that CRA personnel are accessible to consumers.

The FCRA is designed to promote accuracy, fairness, and privacy of information in the files of every consumer reporting agency. To provide consumers the ability to more easily resolve inaccuracies in their credit reports quickly, Congress amended the FCRA (effective September 30, 1997) to require Experian, Equifax, and Trans Union to provide consumers who receive a copy of their credit report with a toll-free telephone number at which personnel are accessible to consumers during normal business hours. "The reality is that consumers never got the access to the consumer reporting agencies that the law guarantees," said Jodie Bernstein, Director of the FTC's Bureau of Consumer Protection. "These cases demonstrate in no uncertain terms that it's time for Equifax, Experian, and Trans Union to pick up the phone and meet their obligations to consumers."

Equifax is based in Atlanta, Georgia; Trans Union is based in Chicago, Illinois; and Experian (formerly, TRW) is an Ohio corporation, with its principal place of business in Orange, California. They are the largest consumer reporting agencies in the nation. According to the FTC's complaints, although all three CRAs had established toll-free telephone numbers for consumers, they violated the accessibility requirement of Section 609(c)(1)(B) since the provision went into effect in September 1997, because a substantial number of consumers have been unable to access the CRAs' personnel when calling the toll-free numbers during normal business hours.

The complaints against Trans Union and Experian allege that more than a million calls to their toll-free numbers since September 1997 received a busy signal or a message indicating that the consumer must call back because all representatives are busy. The complaint against Equifax contains a similar allegation involving hundreds of thousands of calls by consumers to its toll-free numbers. Further, each complaint alleges that a number of callers to the CRAs' toll-free numbers experienced an unreasonable hold time while waiting to speak with CRA personnel during normal business hours.

Finally, the complaints against Equifax and Trans Union allege that each blocked certain incoming telephone calls based upon the location of the call, including, but not limited to, area code. The proposed consent decrees contain specific injunctive provisions that ensure the three CRAs maintain toll-free telephone numbers with personnel accessible to consumers who receive a copy of their credit report. Each of the proposed settlements would require that the CRAs maintain a blocked call rate of no greater than 10 percent and an average hold time of no greater than three minutes and thirty seconds. To measure the CRAs' compliance with these standards, the CRAs will be required to conduct regular audits in accordance with guidelines specified as part of the settlement. Further, the proposed consent decrees would require each of the CRAs to fully comply with Section 609(c)(1)(B) of the FCRA in the future.

Finally, Equifax has agreed to pay $500,000, and Experian and Trans Union both have agreed to pay $1 million, all pursuant to the Commission's authority to collect civil penalties, as a monetary settlement of the charges.

NOTE: A consent decree is for settlement purposes only and does not constitute an admission by the defendant of a law violation. A consent decree is subject to court approval and has the force of law when signed by the judge.

❑ ❑ ❑

The need for credit repair

Given the bureaucratic difficulties of dealing with the credit reporting agencies, it's easy to see how consumers quickly feel overwhelmed and are ready to pay credit repair agencies to take care of things. But the term "credit repair" is really a misnomer. No one can remove accurate and timely negative information from a credit report, except perhaps the creditor. Credit repair clinics prey upon those whose credit bureau reports contain negative information that interferes with their ability to obtain credit. And between bad debt and inaccurate credit bureau reports, credit repair has developed into a major industry abounding with scam artists. Most of the time, these agencies can't do anything you couldn't do for yourself for free.

Credit clinic warning signs

According to the FTC, consumers should beware of credit repair companies that:

- ❑ Want you to pay for credit repair services before any services are provided.
- ❑ Do not tell you your legal rights, and what you can do for yourself for free.
- ❑ Recommend that you do not contact a credit bureau directly.
- ❑ Advise you to dispute all information in your credit report.
- ❑ Advise you to take actions that are illegal, such as creating a new credit identity.

The Credit Repair Organizations Act (see Appendix A for highlights) is a federal law that makes most of these strategies illegal. However, it is too early to tell whether or not the law will be effective in stopping fraudulent practices by credit repair clinics, especially because nonprofit organizations are exempt from the regulations. (If a company can change its status to tax-exempt, it may be able to stay in business.) It is best to acquaint yourself with the basic credit scams, because they're almost sure to reappear in a new guise, regardless of what the law says. The most basic scam takes advantage of the dispute procedure, and this scam is the least affected by the new law. Other common scams are covered in Chapter 8.

Taking advantage of the dispute procedure

The principal method employed by a vast majority of credit repair organizations to improve consumers' credit reports is the dispute procedure available to consumers under Section 611 of the FCRA. This section is designed to provide consumers with a self-help mechanism to correct credit reports that contain inaccurate or incomplete information. Correcting and updating such information benefits creditors as well as consumers by helping to ensure that credit-granting decisions are made on the basis of complete and accurate information reflecting the consumer's probable creditworthiness.

Many consumers who turn to credit repair firms for help have experienced significant credit problems in the past, which they hope to minimize. In the event that the negative information reported about them is accurate and verifiable, FCRA dispute procedures are unlikely to be of help.

Nonetheless, through advertisement and oral representations, credit repair organizations often lead consumers to believe that adverse information in their credit reports can be deleted or modified regardless of its accuracy. Their services are frequently sold on a money-back-guarantee basis, but consumers have reported difficulties in obtaining refunds. The companies may be out of business, lack the funds to pay by the time consumers seek refunds, or simply refuse to honor their guarantees. Credit repair organizations have caused economic injury to credit bureaus as well as to consumers in this regard.

The FCRA states that disputed information must be deleted if it meets any of three criteria: it is inaccurate; it can no longer be verified; or it is obsolete. So in addition to requiring that inaccurate information be removed, the law requires the deletion of disputed information that can no longer be verified or is found to be obsolete.

This is important to note, because experience has shown that some credit grantors do not verify information more than 25 months old. Their reason is that the Equal Credit Opportunity Act requires creditors to maintain written documentation for a minimum of 25 months. Some time after that period, creditors purge the information. Thus, disputed information is, in fact, frequently deleted from the credit report because it can no longer be verified.

Credit bureaus are required by Section 611 of the FCRA to reinvestigate disputed information within a reasonable period of time and to delete information that they cannot verify. A credit bureau may delete accurate information from a consumer's credit bureau report because it is overwhelmed by disputes generated by credit repair organizations or because creditors fail to respond promptly to verification requests.

In the past, certain credit repair firms have attempted to deluge credit bureaus with numerous sequential disputes. They would send the identical dispute to the credit bureau six times—once every three days. The credit bureaus were not set up to handle such a strategy but attempted to do so using outdated procedures.

When a dispute was received, it would be given to one of 50 consumer relations clerks, who would in turn generate a consumer dispute verification form. The form was then submitted to the source of the information for a reply. Three days later an identical dispute would arrive, and the same process would be followed. The credit repair companies alleged that the disputes were not being returned to the credit bureau because the creditor (source) was confused. Perhaps he had returned one dispute form but not another, and as a result, the information was purged from the files.

The bureaus used two avenues to combat this situation. The first involved placing a coded message on the credit report, which, for a period of 30 calendar days, depicted the identification and relationship of the consumer with a particular consumer relations clerk, thereby avoiding subsequent frivolous or irrelevant disputes. Avenue number two involved the deletion of information that was not returned from the source within 20 working days; however, if it was later returned, it was added to the file and treated as new information. This procedure appears to have been effective in combating such strategies used by credit repair companies.

The development of the credit repair industry is a relatively recent phenomenon, fueled by the tremendous increase in the use of consumer credit over the last 30 years. The need for credit repair arose both because consumers found themselves in legitimate trouble and because credit reporting agencies often mismanaged the information they sold to creditors.

The strategies employed by these clinics to remove legitimate information range from those I've just described—taking advantage of legal loopholes and bureaucratic inefficiency—to creating new credit identities and other questionable tactics. The credit bureaus have fought the clinics through state and federal legislative agencies. Laws have been passed regulating the practices of credit repair clinics in 35 states, and in 1996, the Credit Repair Organizations Act was passed at the federal level. The chapters that follow examine some of the more outrageous and dangerous scams that credit clinics have run, and provide an overview of laws governing credit repair practices.

Chapter 12

Credit Repair Scams

"Got bad credit? Bankruptcy, foreclosures, repossessions? No problem," declare newspaper and television ads promising to fix your credit record or get you credit cards and car loans. With millions of consumers struggling to overcome spotty credit histories, hundreds of companies have sprung up to take advantage of their predicament. Many of them, according to law enforcement agencies and the Better Business Bureau, are rip-offs.

Their "services" typically include blanket disputes of credit report items in hopes of having some or all of the negative items removed, or advising or assisting you in creating a new credit file or identity. Sometimes they just want you to join the company and be part of the multilevel marketing scheme.

Whether you hire such a firm, or decide to work for one, beware! The bottom line on credit repair, according to the nonprofit National Foundation for Consumer Credit in Silver Spring, Md., is, again, that credit repair companies cannot (legally) do anything you cannot do yourself.

Under the Federal Fair Credit Reporting Act (FCRA), the credit bureaus must tell consumers what their credit files contain, if they ask. If the information is inaccurate, the consumer can challenge it free of charge. The credit bureau has 30 days to confirm the data or remove it from the file. But if legal judgments, bankruptcies, or other pieces of your credit history are valid, nothing can change them. Still, consumers line up at the clinics, and they often get taken to the cleaners. A few examples of scams and typical experiences follow.

Take the case of Etta Grant, a Mineral Springs, N.C., hairdresser who met with a Charlotte salesman for Nationwide Credit Corporation and agreed to pay $1,197 for services. She put $200 down and wrote six additional postdated checks (for $166.17 each) to be cashed once a month.

Nationwide cashed three of the postdated checks, then deposited the fourth one early. There wasn't enough money in Grant's account yet to cover it, so her credit record actually got worse when it and other checks she had written bounced. The attorney general's office and Grant's private attorney were unable to get a refund from Nationwide. By 1994, the North Carolina Attorney General's Office was investigating 15 complaints against Nationwide Credit and two other companies at Nationwide's address.

According to the National Center for Financial Education, consumers nationwide and U.S. servicepersons overseas lost more than $50 million over a five-year period as a result of hiring fly-by-night operators to "fix" personal credit files, with little or no results. A typical scenario follows: XYZ Company comes into town and launches a major advertising campaign. It claims that it will remove everything from your credit report for $500. Within 30 days it has enrolled 1,000 people and skipped town—to the tune of a cool half-million dollars. Not bad for a month's work and some advertising.

Many such scams have been perpetrated by rings of proficient con artists. More often, however, the credit consultant begins with perfectly good intentions. What happens is usually something like this:

Bill Mooch spends his late nights watching cable TV shows about how to get into real estate with no money down or borrow millions of dollars on his credit cards. One night he sees a program about the dynamic opportunity in credit consulting. He calls the toll-free number, pays his $129, breezes through the course, and becomes a "professional credit consultant"—certificate and everything.

After that he sends in more money to become an associate. For only $1,000 more, he gets a briefcase and a set of business cards. Now he's really in business. He begins a massive advertising campaign. His credit cards are now at their limits. Then it happens. Money starts pouring in. He's got more business than he can handle. At $500 to $1,000 per client, Bill is on a serious roll.

Three months later the phone calls from the first clients start coming in: "I haven't heard anything on my case. My credit is still messed up! I want my money back."

Bill freaks out. A week later, Bill and his wife decide to take a vacation—a permanent one. "What the heck, we can afford it," they decide.

In another instance, a credit consultant in Orange County, Calif., made a fortune by obtaining credit card applications from creditworthy individuals for a fee. Here's how it worked: The consultant would go to firms who wanted to get creditworthy individuals to accept their credit cards. He made deals with oil companies, department stores, banks, car rental firms, and many others to pay so much for each valid credit application he turned in.

To put this on a wholesale plan where he could reap $20 or more per application, he went to the county records office and got the names and the mortgage holders of homeowners in the area. He called the homeowners, identifying himself as a representative of the mortgage holder on the property and stated that he needed a credit update. He would proceed to get all the information on a current application form and inquire as to which credit cards the people already held. All the companies he was representing whose credit cards the consumers didn't already have received these filled-out forms as applications for credit cards. He informed the homeowners that he had made arrangements with some companies to issue credit cards to them, that there was no obligation on their part to use them, but that they could come in handy in emergencies. Most people were amenable to this and raised no fuss. The consultant grossed more than $100,000 in a four-week period.

Changing your identity

Among the most notorious and dangerous of credit repair scams is the creation of a new credit file. In the past, the scam has worked like this: A credit repair company obtains a listing of recent bankruptcy filings from the public records. The company sends letters to the recent filers full of dire warnings about their inability to get any kind of credit, perhaps for as long as 10 years—no credit cards, car loans, personal loans, or mortgages.

However, for a fee, the credit repair company promises to help by providing instructions on how to create a new credit identity. After paying the fee, the consumers receive instructions on applying for an Employer Identification Number (EIN) from the Internal Revenue Service. The credit repair company advises them to use the new employer ID in place of their Social Security numbers when applying for credit. It also advises them to use a new mailing address (usually that of a relative or friend).

Later, when a bank or department store runs a credit check on the alias, it turns up nothing, especially if the name has been changed. That is because the credit bureaus have no way of linking a fake ID with the real individual using it.

Credit One Services of Fort Bragg, Calif., is the largest such operation uncovered so far. Before being shut down in April 1992, with the arrest of its owner, John P. Ruggeri, and his wife, Nancy, Credit One had sold its $39 kits to 20,000 people.

In March 1992, the IRS put out an alert on Credit One Services, warning that anyone who got involved in the scheme could face tax fraud charges. The agency had noticed a rise in mismatched Social Security numbers that it could not explain. At the same time, the Better Business Bureau alerted the IRS to complaints about Credit One. The Los Angeles City Attorney's Office filed criminal charges, and the FTC, the State Department of Consumer Affairs, and the Attorney General's Office filed civil lawsuits seeking fines. The U.S. Postal Service seized the Ruggeris' mail, and the FTC froze their bank accounts.

John and Nancy Ruggeri pleaded no contest to criminal violations of the state's credit repair laws and business code. Nancy Ruggeri was sentenced to 30 days in jail and 30 days under house arrest. John Ruggeri was sentenced to five months in the Los Angeles County jail.

The Federal Trade Commission has frequently warned consumers to be on the alert for unscrupulous credit repair companies that offer to create a new credit file by instructing individuals to obtain an EIN from the IRS. An EIN, which resembles a Social Security number, is used by businesses for reporting financial information to the IRS and the Social Security Administration. The bulletin states that these credit repair companies are instructing individuals with bad credit to use the EINs in place of their Social Security numbers, along with a new mailing address.

The law catches up

According to the IRS, people who change their Social Security numbers are cheating themselves of future Social Security payments for the years they work. Of more immediate concern, though, is that if your actions are determined to be fraudulent, you could be criminally liable for falsifying tax records. Credit repair companies that promote such schemes could be liable for participating in a conspiracy to defraud the government.

Here's what the FTC says: "It is a federal crime to make any false statements on a loan or credit application, which the credit repair company may advise you to do. It is a federal crime to misrepresent your Social Security number. It is also a federal crime to obtain an EIN from the IRS under false pretenses."

As if that weren't enough, the commission also warns that you could be charged with mail or wire fraud if you use the mail or telephone to apply for credit and provide false information. And you may be guilty of civil fraud under many state laws.

As of 1996, it is illegal to advise consumers to alter his or her identification to hide accurate information in a credit report. Section 404 of the Credit Repair Organizations Act of 1996 states:

No person may make any statement, or counsel or advise any consumer to make any statement, the intended effect of which is to alter the consumer's identification to prevent the display of the consumer's credit record, history or rating for the purpose of concealing adverse information that is accurate and not obsolete to any consumer reporting agency; any person who has extended credit to the person; or any person to whom the consumer has applied or is applying for an extension of credit.

The Credit Repair Organizations Act also addresses other major problems with credit repair clinics; it prohibits clinics from accepting payment for services before they are performed; and it requires the clinics to give you a statement explaining your credit reporting rights under state and federal law. (For more complete information, see Appendix A.)

In April of 1996 the FTC and 10 state attorneys general launched "Operation Payback," a federal-state crackdown on fraudulent credit repair telemarketers. Included were specific actions against companies such as Giving You Credit and Partners in Vision International, Inc., of San Diego, Calif., and Clear Your Credit, Inc., of Chicago, Ill. Their multilevel marketing plan sold credit repair services through representatives who earned commissions on their sales and for recruiting new sales reps. Among the tactics used by the defendants was to falsely claim that the FCRA requires deletion of an entire negative entry if it is not 100-percent accurate. Other "Operation Payback" actions were conducted in Illinois, Indiana, Massachusetts, Missouri, North Carolina, Ohio, Tennessee, Washington, and Wisconsin that resulted in fines and cease and desist orders against 17 credit repair companies.

Credit repair goes high-tech

The credit repair industry has been as quick as any to get onto the Internet to market its services. The package may look different in cyberspace, but the contents tend to be the same, and consumers should watch out. For example, in March of 1996, the FTC came to a settlement with two New York City law firms that were behind a deceptive advertisement posted on 3,000 Internet news groups.

In this case, the defendants posted an ad that stated, in part: "...Our LAW FIRM offers direct guaranteed effective credit restoration services by experienced attorneys....We have successfully facilitated the removal of Late Payments, Charge-Offs, Foreclosures, Repossessions, Collection Accounts, Loan Defaults, Tax Liens, Judgments and Bankruptcies from our clients' reports. WE GUARANTEE THAT YOUR CREDIT CAN BE RESTORED!"

The defendants charged a minimum of $500, with fees ranging from $125 to $700 for each item challenged.

The FTC charged that the defendants misrepresented their success rate for improving consumers' credit reports and misrepresented their ability to have derogatory information removed from credit reports regardless of the age or accuracy of the information.

Chapter 13

Identification Theft

A thief goes through trash to find discarded receipts and then uses your account numbers illegally.

A dishonest clerk makes an extra imprint from your credit or charge card and uses it to make personal charges.

You respond to a mailing asking you to call a long-distance number for a free trip or bargain-priced travel package. You're told you must join a travel club first and you're asked for your account number so you can be billed. Charges you didn't make are added to your bill, and you never get your trip.

❑ ❑ ❑

Credit and charge card fraud costs cardholders and issuers hundreds of millions of dollars each year. It's not always possible to prevent credit or charge card fraud from happening. There are a few steps you can take, though, to make it more difficult for a crook to capture your card or card numbers.

Guarding against fraud

Here are some tips to help protect yourself from credit and charge card fraud.

Do:

- ❑ Sign your cards as soon as they arrive.
- ❑ Carry your cards separately from your wallet, in a zippered compartment, a business card holder, or another small pouch.
- ❑ Keep a record of your account numbers, their expiration dates, and the phone number and address of each company in a secure place.
- ❑ Keep an eye on your card during the transaction, and get it back as quickly as possible.
- ❑ Void incorrect receipts.
- ❑ Destroy carbons.
- ❑ Save receipts to compare with billing statements.
- ❑ Open bills promptly and reconcile accounts monthly, just as you do your checking account.
- ❑ Report any questionable charges promptly and in writing to the card issuer.
- ❑ Notify card companies in advance of a change in address.

Don't:

- ❑ Lend your cards to anyone.
- ❑ Leave cards or receipts lying around.
- ❑ Sign a blank receipt. When you sign a receipt, draw a line through any blank spaces above the total.
- ❑ Write your account number on a postcard or the outside of an envelope.
- ❑ Give out your account number over the phone unless you're making the call to a company you know is reputable. If you have questions about a company, check it out with your local consumer protection office or Better Business Bureau.

Reporting losses and fraud

If you lose your credit or charge cards or realize they've been lost or stolen, immediately call the issuer(s). Many companies have toll-free numbers and 24-hour service to deal with such emergencies. By law, once you report the loss or theft, you have no further responsibility for unauthorized charges. In any event, your maximum liability under federal law is $50 per card.

If you suspect fraud, you may be asked to sign a statement under oath that you did not make the purchase(s) in question.

What to do if your identity is stolen

"I don't remember opening that credit card account. And I certainly didn't buy those items I'm being billed for."

Maybe you never opened that account, but someone else did—someone who used your name and personal information to commit fraud. When an imposter co-opts your name, your Social Security number, your credit card number, or some other piece of your personal information for their use—in short, when someone appropriates your personal information without your knowledge—it's a crime, pure and simple.

The biggest problem is that you may not know your identity's been stolen until you notice that something's amiss. You may get bills for a credit card account you never opened, your credit report may include debts you never knew you had, a billing cycle may pass without your receiving a statement, or you may see charges on your bills that you didn't sign for, didn't authorize, and don't know anything about.

Steps to take

If someone has stolen your identity, the Federal Trade Commission recommends that you take three actions immediately.

First, contact the fraud departments of each of the three major credit bureaus. Tell them to flag your file with a fraud alert including a statement that creditors should get your permission before opening any new accounts in your name.

At the same time, ask the credit bureaus for copies of your credit reports. Credit bureaus must give you a free copy of your report if it is inaccurate because of fraud. Review your reports carefully to make sure no additional fraudulent accounts have been opened in your name or unauthorized changes made to your existing accounts. In a few months, order new copies of your reports to verify your corrections and changes, and to make sure no new fraudulent activity has occurred.

Here are the telephone numbers for the fraud departments of the Big Three credit bureaus:

Equifax
(800) 525-6285
(800) 685-1111

Experian
(888) EXPERIAN (397-3742)

Trans Union
(800) 680-7289
(800) 916-8800

Second, contact the creditors for any accounts that have been tampered with or opened fraudulently. Speak with someone in the security or fraud department, and follow up in writing. Following up with a letter is one of the procedures spelled out in the Fair Credit Billing Act for resolving errors on credit billing statements, including charges that you have not made.

Third, file a report with your local police or the police in the community where the identity theft took place. Keep a copy of the police report in case your creditors need proof of the crime.

Take control

Although identity thieves can wreak havoc on your personal finances, there are some things you can do to take control of the situation. Here's how to handle some of the most common forms of identity theft.

If an identity thief has stolen your mail for access to new credit cards, bank and credit card statements, pre-approved credit offers, tax information, or falsified change-of-address forms, he or she has committed a crime. Report it to your local postal inspector.

If you discover that an identity thief has changed the billing address on an existing credit card account, close the account. When you open a new account, ask that a password be used before any inquiries or changes can be made on the account. Avoid using easily available information, such as your mother's maiden name, your birthdate, the last four digits of your Social Security number, your phone number, or a series of consecutive numbers. Avoid the same information and numbers when you create a Personal Identification Number (PIN).

If you have reason to believe that an identity thief has accessed your bank accounts, checking account, or ATM card, close the accounts immediately. When you open new accounts, insist on password-only access. If your checks have been stolen or misused, issue a stop payment on them. If your ATM card has been lost, stolen, or otherwise compromised, cancel the card and get another with a new PIN.

If an identity thief has established new phone or wireless service in your name and is making unauthorized calls that appear to come from (and are billed to) your cellular phone, or is using your calling card and PIN, contact your service provider immediately to cancel the account and calling card. Get new accounts and new PINs.

If it appears that someone is using your Social Security number when applying for a job, get in touch with the Social Security Administration to verify the accuracy of your reported earnings and that your name is reported correctly. Call (800) 772-1213 to check your Social Security Statement.

In addition, the Social Security Administration may issue you a new Social Security number at your request if, after trying to resolve the problems brought on by identity theft, you continue to experience problems. Consider this option carefully. A new Social Security number may not resolve your identity theft problems. It may actually create new problems. For example, a new Social Security number does not necessarily ensure a new credit record, because credit bureaus may combine the credit records from your old number with those from your new number. Even when the old credit information is not associated with your new Social Security number, the absence of any credit history under your new number may make it more difficult for you to get credit. Also, there's no guarantee that a new Social Security number wouldn't also be misused by an identity thief.

If you suspect that your name or Social Security number is being used by an identity thief to get a driver's license, report it to your Department of Motor Vehicles. Also, if your state uses your Social Security number as your driver's license number, ask to substitute another number.

If your wallet or purse is lost or stolen, the Federal Trade Commission suggests that you:

- ❑ File a report with the police immediately. Get a copy in case your bank, credit card company or insurance company needs proof of the crime.
- ❑ Cancel each credit and charge card. Get new cards with new account numbers. Call the fraud departments of the major credit reporting agencies and ask them to put a "fraud alert" on your account and add a "victim's statement" to your file requesting that creditors contact you before opening new accounts in your name.
- ❑ Ask the credit bureaus for copies of your credit reports. Review your reports carefully to make sure no additional fraudulent accounts have been opened in your name or unauthorized changes made to your existing accounts. In a few months, order new copies of your reports to verify your corrections and changes, and to make sure no new fraudulent activity has occurred.

- ❑ Report the loss to your bank if your wallet or purse contained bank account information, including account numbers, ATM cards, or checks. Cancel checking and savings accounts and open new ones. Stop payments on outstanding checks.
- ❑ Get a new ATM card, account number, and Personal Identification Number (PIN) or password.
- ❑ Report your missing driver's license to the department of motor vehicles. If your state uses your Social Security number as your driver's license number, ask to substitute another number.
- ❑ Change the locks on your home and car if your keys were taken. Don't give an identity thief access to even more personal property and information.

If you've been a victim of identity theft, file a complaint with the FTC by contacting the FTC's Identity Theft Hotline by telephone: toll-free at (877) ID-THEFT (438-4338) or TDD at (202) 326-2502; by mail at Identity Theft Clearinghouse, Federal Trade Commission, 600 Pennsylvania Avenue, NW, Washington, D.C. 20580; or online at *www.consumer.gov/idtheft.* Ask for a copy of *ID Theft: When Bad Things Happen to Your Good Name,* a free comprehensive consumer guide to help you guard against and recover from identity theft.

Identity Theft and Assumption Deterrence Act

In October 1998, Congress passed the Identity Theft and Assumption Deterrence Act of 1998 (Identity Theft Act) to address the problem of identity theft. Specifically, the Act amended 18 U.S.C. § 1028 to make it a federal crime when anyone knowingly transfers or uses, without lawful authority, a means of identification of another person with the intent to commit, or to aid or abet, any unlawful activity that constitutes a violation of Federal law, or that constitutes a felony under any applicable State or local law.

Violations of the Act are investigated by federal investigative agencies such as the U.S. Secret Service, the FBI, and the U.S. Postal Inspection Service and prosecuted by the Department of Justice. Here are a few examples of reported cases of identity theft.

❑❑❑

FTC Cracks Down On Internet Credit Rip Off

To combat the latest wrinkle in hi-tech fraud on the Internet, the Federal Trade Commission has charged three individuals and eight businesses with billing or debiting consumers' credit card accounts for unordered or fictitious Internet services. The FTC alleges the defendants repeatedly placed charges on consumers' credit and debit cards for Internet entertainment services they had not ordered and did not want. Some of the consumers who were billed didn't even own computers. When consumers tried to contest the charges, they were met by confusing voice mail messages, anonymous Internet sites and a maze of mail-drops. At the FTC's request, a U.S. District Court judge has issued a temporary restraining order, appointed a temporary receiver for two of the companies and frozen their assets, pending a further hearing. The agency will ask the court to halt the bogus billing practices permanently and to order consumer redress or disgorgement.

The FTC named Kenneth H. Taves, aka Kenneth Till, Teresa Callei Taves, Gary Mittman, all of California, and their companies (J. K. Publications, Inc., MJD Service Corp., and Net Options, Inc.) in its complaint. The complaint alleges that the defendants also use the business names Netfill, N–Bill, Webtel, and Online Billing.

The FTC alleged that the defendants obtained consumer credit and debit card account numbers without consumers' knowledge or approval, and billed or debited consumers' accounts for services the consumers had not ordered, did not want, and in some cases, couldn't use because they had no computer. The charge item on the bill contained the name of one of the various businesses and an 800 phone number. Consumers who called the number to get the charge removed from their credit card got a busy signal, no answer, or a recording directing them to enter their credit card number to discuss charges. They often were unable to get through to a person to discuss the charges. Consumers, many of whom were billed repeatedly over successive months, appealed to credit card companies for help, but were told by them that they could not block future charges to the cards. Many consumers canceled their credit card accounts to avoid the charges, the FTC alleged. The FTC has asked the court to permanently bar the illegal billing practices and award redress to consumers.

❑ ❑ ❑

San Diego County Woman Sentenced To Federal Prison For Stealing Identity Of University Professor

Theresa Marie Thompson-Snow, of Chula Vista, Calif., was sentenced to 16 months in federal prison for using a stolen Social Security number to obtain thousands of dollars in credit and then filing for bankruptcy in the name of her victim. During the sentencing hearing, Assistant United States Attorney Ranee Katzenstein argued that Thompson-Snow had continued to engage in fraudulent conduct while awaiting sentencing. After the sentencing, Judge Marshall immediately remanded the defendant into custody, finding that Thompson-Snow had not been "forthcoming" with the court. Judge Marshall also said she "could not find that she [Thompson-Snow] would not continue to be involved with illegal activity." In addition to the prison term, Judge Marshall imposed restitution in the amount of $13,928 and ordered the defendant to pay a $5,000 criminal fine.

Thompson-Snow pleaded guilty to three counts of false representation of a Social Security number and one count of bankruptcy fraud. By pleading guilty, Thompson-Snow admitted that she assumed the identity of another woman with a similar name in order to obtain loans that Thompson-Snow was not qualified to receive. The defendant, who was a licensed notary public at the time and has since been employed as a paralegal, defaulted on the loans. In January 1997, Thompson-Snow sought to avoid the consequences of the defaults by fraudulently filing for bankruptcy.

The FBI began investigating the case after it was contacted by the victim, Theresa Mae Thompson, an English professor at Valdosta State University (Georgia). Professor Thompson had graduated from a college in Arizona that the defendant also briefly attended, and both women had received student loans that were administered through the same company. Due to a computer mix-up, documents belonging to Professor Thompson, which included her Social Security number, were sent to the defendant in 1995. Shortly thereafter, Professor Thompson began receiving telephone calls from companies that she had never heard of claiming she owed them large sums of money.

❑ ❑ ❑

268-Count Indictment Charges 9 Nigerian Nationals with Nationwide Credit Identity Takeover Scheme Linked to Heroin Distribution, Forgery, and Tax Fraud Conspiracies

On July 12, 1999, Queens District Attorney Richard A. Brown, joined by New York City Police Commissioner Howard Safir and Lee R. Heath, Inspector in Charge, United States Postal Inspection Service, New York Division, announced today the indictment of nine Nigerian nationals in connection with a sophisticated nationwide credit identity takeover scheme aimed at victimizing more than 1,300 individuals in 20 states and many of our country's largest credit and banking institutions; the sale and distribution of large quantities of heroin; the forgery of drivers licenses, Social Security cards, credit cards and checks; and the filing of fraudulent federal, state and local tax returns.

District Attorney Brown said, "The joint investigation leading to the indictment began as an investigation into heroin trafficking. Over time, and as the result of court-authorized eavesdropping and other investigative methods, it was discovered that, in addition to heroin trafficking, the defendants were engaged in various fraudulent activities, including a sophisticated series of identity takeover schemes and a conspiracy to forge financial documents and file fraudulent tax returns."

According to the 268-count indictment, in addition to the undercover heroin sales, beginning in the spring of 1996 and until April 1999, defendants Ayodele Peters, his wife Yewande Peters, and others allegedly stole more than $1.4 million dollars from 20 banks and credit card institutions in Maryland, Delaware, Illinois, New York, Colorado, and other states in a sophisticated identity takeover conspiracy. It is charged that defendant Ayodele Peters, with the help of his wife and Adebiyi Otulaja, among others, purchased copies of rental car agreements from a former employee of a car rental agency in Warwick, Rhode Island, for $20 each. Armed with the names, addresses, Social Security numbers, credit card account numbers, and copies of the drivers licenses of hundreds of legitimate citizens obtained from the rental agreements, the defendants are alleged to have obtained additional information about the victims' bank accounts and credit card accounts. During the course of the conspiracy, the defendants then allegedly opened approximately 80 new bank accounts and began transferring cash advances from legitimate cardholders' accounts to the accounts they had established using additional fictitious or stolen names and other information. They then would withdraw the money from the accounts they had created. In some instances it is alleged that the defendants made direct cash withdrawals from victims' accounts or used stolen or forged convenience checks written on their accounts.

District Attorney Brown said, "Our investigation revealed that the defendant Ayodele Peters and his co-conspirators had accumulated financial and personal information, including mothers' maiden names, of approximately 1,300 legitimate citizens from across the country, which gave the defendants access to about $10 million dollars in credit. Although banks cover these kinds of financial losses, the real loss to the victim is the loss of his or her credit rating and good name. There is also a personally invasive quality to this kind of fraud that causes victims a great deal of distress. It takes months—often years—to undo the damage done to the reputations of the victims of identity fraud and to restore their credit status and, of course, the monetary loss suffered by the banks and financial institutions is passed along to their customers in higher interest rates and fees."

"In addition," said the District Attorney, "the indictment charges that defendant Derrick Rountree, an accountant who had offices in the Jess Center at 11 Snyder Avenue in Brooklyn, conspired with Bola Adeola, Ayodele Peters, Olusola Ashaye, Adebiyi Otulaja, and Abiodun Oguntoyinbo to create forged Social Security cards, checks, drivers licenses, and State Department immigration visa applications in order to:

supply Ayodele Peters and others with identification to open fraudulent bank accounts;

allow aliens living in the New York area to file multiple copies of immigration lottery applications; and

furnish illegal aliens with the documentation necessary to obtain employment.

It is also charged that Rountree conspired with said defendants to electronically file federal, state, and local tax returns with fraudulent W-2 forms and false dependent Social Security numbers claiming refunds due to the defendants—refunds which were promptly paid by the tax authorities."

All of the defendants in the case were convicted, including the leader, who was sentenced to 10 years in prison.

❑ ❑ ❑

Hoax Targets Elderly African Americans

"Apply for Newly Approved Slave Reparations! Claim $5,000 in Social Security Reimbursements!"

Flyers with these instructions, circulating in many southern and midwestern African-American communities, are attempting to trick people into revealing personal identifying information that could, in turn, cost them money or damage their credit ratings.

The flyers, distributed in churches or placed on the windshields of parked cars or bulletin boards in senior centers and nursing homes, claim that African Americans born before 1928 may be eligible for slave reparations under a so-called "Slave Reparation Act" and that those born between 1917 and 1926 can apply for Social Security funds they are due because of a "fix" in the Social Security system.

According to law enforcement officials, the claims are false. They are being made by skilled identity thieves who are asking people to reveal their name, address, phone number, birthdate, and Social Security number in order to access their credit cards or open accounts under their names without their permission or knowledge.

If you receive a flyer promoting slave reparations or Social Security reimbursements, the Federal Trade Commission encourages you to report it to your local law enforcement agency or state attorney general, the Social Security Administration or the FTC at its toll-free Identity Theft Hotline (877-ID-THEFT [877-438-4338]).

Can you minimize your risk of identity theft? The FTC says by managing your personal information wisely, cautiously and with increased sensitivity, you may be able to thwart an identity thief. The federal agency recommends that you:

- ❑ Never reveal your personal identifying information unless you know exactly who you're dealing with and how it will be used.
- ❑ Verify the details with any government agency that's involved in an offer. You can find the phone number for every government agency in the blue pages of your telephone book.

- ❑ Read all your bills carefully. Call your creditors to dispute any charge you didn't make or authorize.
- ❑ Order a copy of your credit report every year from each of the three major credit reporting agencies to verify that your credit information is accurate.

Chapter 14

Choosing a Credit Counselor

Living paycheck to paycheck? Worried about debt collectors? Can't seem to develop a workable budget, let alone save money for retirement? If this sounds familiar, you may want to consider the services of a credit counseling agency. Usually nonprofit, these agencies work with you to solve your financial problems—sometimes for free. Credit counseling agencies may offer educational materials and workshops, or help you develop a budget. Many agencies offer services nationwide through local offices or the Internet. Look under "credit counseling" in your telephone directory or an Internet search engine.

Debt repayment plans

If your financial difficulties arise from too much debt or an inability to repay your debts, a credit counseling agency may work out a debt repayment plan for you. In these plans, you deposit money each month with the credit counseling agency. Your deposits are used to pay your creditors according to a payment schedule the counselor develops with you.

You may also have to agree not to apply for—or use—any additional credit while you're participating in the program.

A debt repayment plan does not erase your credit history. Under the Fair Credit Reporting Act, accurate information about your accounts can stay on your credit report for up to seven years. A bankruptcy can stay on your report for 10 years. In addition, your creditors will continue to report information about accounts that are handled through a debt repayment plan.

Choosing an agency

If you want to work with a credit counseling agency, interview several. Some questions to ask regarding services, fees, and repayment plans follow. Check with your state attorney general, local consumer protection agency, and the Better Business Bureau to find out if consumers have filed complaints about the provider you are considering. Any reputable credit counseling agency should send you free information about itself and its services without requiring you to provide any details about your situation. If not, consider that a red flag and go elsewhere for help.

Services and fees

- ❑ What services do you offer?
- ❑ Do you have educational materials? If so, will you send them to me? Are they free? Can I access them on the Internet?
- ❑ In addition to helping me solve my immediate problem, will you help me develop a plan for avoiding problems in the future?
- ❑ What are your fees? Do I have to pay anything before you can help me? Are there monthly fees? What's the basis for the fees?
- ❑ What is the source of your funding?
- ❑ Will I have a formal written agreement or contract with you?
- ❑ How soon can you take my case?
- ❑ Who regulates, oversees, and/or licenses your agency? Is your agency audited?

- ❑ Will I work with one counselor or several?
- ❑ What are the qualifications of your counselors? Are they accredited or certified? If not, how are they trained?
- ❑ What assurance do I have that information about me (including my address and phone number) will be kept confidential?

Repayment plan

- ❑ How much do I have to owe to use your services?
- ❑ How do you determine the amount of my payment? What happens if this is more than I can afford?
- ❑ How does your debt repayment plan work? How will I know my creditors have received payments? Is client money put in a separate account from operating funds?
- ❑ How often can I get status reports on my accounts? Can I get access to my accounts online or by phone?
- ❑ Can you get my creditors to lower or eliminate interest and finance charges or waive late fees?
- ❑ Is a debt repayment plan my only option?
- ❑ What if I can't maintain the agreed-upon plan?
- ❑ What debts will be excluded from the debt repayment plan?
- ❑ Will you help me plan for payment of these debts?
- ❑ Who will help me if I have problems with my accounts or creditors?
- ❑ How secure is the information I provide to you?

Conclusion

Getting Help

The various consumer credit laws presented in this book are enforced by federal, state, and local agencies. If you would like further information or have a particular problem you would like addressed, you can contact the appropriate agencies.

If your problem is with a credit repair company, credit bureau, debt collector, consumer finance company, or retail department store, contact:

Division of Credit Practices
Federal Trade Commission
Washington, D.C. 20580
www.ftc.gov

State and local consumer protection offices resolve individual consumer complaints, conduct informational and educational programs, and enforce consumer protection and fraud laws. Local offices can be particularly helpful for both prepurchase information and complaint handling, because they are often familiar with local businesses and laws. Check your local telephone directory's white pages in the government section for state attorney general, consumer protection division, or consumer affairs division. Your city attorney or district attorney office's fraud division may also be helpful.

Private organizations

The Better Business Bureau assists consumers by investigating disputes with companies and providing consumer mediation and arbitration services. Check your white pages under Better Business Bureau or contact:

Council of Better Business Bureaus, Inc.
4200 Wilson Blvd.
Arlington, VA 22203
www.bbb.org

The Consumer Credit Counseling Service assists consumers who have problems in paying their bills (but are not yet in collection). Contact:

National Foundation for Consumer Credit, Inc.
8611 2nd Ave., Suite 100
Silver Spring, MD 20910
(800) 388-CCCS
www.nfcc.org

Associated Credit Bureaus, Inc., a trade organization, offers a free brochure titled *Consumers, Credit Bureaus and The Fair Credit Reporting Act.* Contact:

Associated Credit Bureaus, Inc.
1090 Vermont Ave., NW, Suite 200
Washington, D.C. 20005-4905
www.acb-credit.com

Appendix A

Summary of Federal Laws Governing Consumer Credit Reporting and Repair

Fair Credit Reporting Act

This act, effective since 1971, gives consumers the following rights:

- To know what credit information is held that relates to them, without charge, if they've been denied credit based on a credit report within 60 days.
- To have a reasonably accurate and complete file.
- To know who has received a report about them in the past six months and who has received a report for employment purposes within the past two years.
- To have information pertaining to them that they dispute reverified and corrected or removed if inaccurate or unverifiable. If there are changes in information reported, the credit bureau must send an updated report to credit grantors who have received a report about the consumer in the last year, or to employers who have received a report within the last two years.

- To place a statement in the credit reporting company's records if they continue to dispute the accuracy of an item after reverification.
- To not have adverse information kept or reported for more than seven years, or up to 10 years for bankruptcies.

The 1996 update to the FCRA (effective October 1, 1997):

- Permits credit bureaus to supply information antedating the request by more than seven or 10 years if the consumer is applying for a loan or insurance of $150,000 or more, or if he or she is applying for a job paying more than $75,000 annually. (The qualifying amounts under the old law were $50,000 and $20,000 respectively.)
- Requires employers seeking credit reports on current or prospective employees to obtain the employee's or applicant's written permission to receive the report. This permission must be signed separately.
- Stipulates that credit bureaus must share corrections to an individual consumer's record with other credit bureaus.
- Requires credit bureaus to establish reasonable procedures to prevent disputed information from being reinserted into files unless the supplier of the information certifies that it is correct. If information is reinserted into a credit file, the credit bureau must notify the consumer and give the name, address and phone of the information supplier.
- Requires creditors and other suppliers of information to promptly investigate and, if necessary, correct disputed information, whether it is brought to them by the consumer or the credit bureau. Corrections must be sent to all major credit bureaus to which the disputed information was reported.

- ❑ Requires credit bureaus to show consumers who request their reports the names of anyone or any business that has requested a credit report on the consumer in the past year (or two years, if the inquiry was made by an employer).
- ❑ Limits charges for consumer credit reports to $8, adjusted annually for inflation. Some states have laws stipulating lower prices for residents.
- ❑ Requires credit bureaus to send reports free of charge, upon request, to consumers who have been turned down for credit within the past 60 days; to persons who are unemployed and intend to apply for employment within 60 days; persons who receive welfare payments; or persons who believe they are victims of credit fraud.
- ❑ Requires credit bureaus to provide toll-free numbers that consumers may call to block their files from prescreening for credit offers. (This is called "opting-out.")
- ❑ Requires the bureaus to share requests received from consumers with each other.
- ❑ Requires bureaus to offer toll-free numbers consumers may call to ask questions when they are denied credit based on information contained in the report.

Credit Repair Organizations Act

The Credit Repair Organizations Act, enacted in 1996, was passed to ensure that prospective buyers of credit repair services are provided with information to make an informed decision regarding the purchase of such services and to protect the public from unfair or deceptive advertising or business practices. It prohibits the following:

No person may make any statement, or counsel any consumer to make any statement, that is untrue or misleading with respect to the consumer's creditworthiness, credit standing or credit capacity, to any (a) consumer reporting agency, (b,i) person who has extended credit to the consumer or (b,ii) person to whom the consumer is applying for an extension of credit.

No person may make any statement, or counsel or advise any consumer to make any statement, the intended effect of which is to alter the consumer's identification to prevent display of the consumer's credit record, history, or rating for the purpose of concealing adverse information that is accurate and not obsolete.

No credit repair organization may charge or receive any money or other valuable consideration for the performance of any service which the credit repair organization has agreed to perform, until the service is fully performed.

No credit repair organization may provide any services to any consumer until a written and dated contract for the purchase of services has been signed by the consumer. The contract must include, in writing, the terms and conditions of payment, including the total amount of all payments to be made by the consumer to the credit repair organization or to any other person. The contract must also give a full and detailed description of services to be performed including all guarantees of performance and an estimate of the date by which performance of services shall be complete or the length of time necessary to perform the services.

Requires that the contract include the credit repair organization's name, principal business address and a conspicuous statement in bold face type that reads "You may cancel this contract without penalty or obligation at any time before midnight of the third business day after the date on which you signed the contract. See the attached notice of cancellation form for an explanation of this right."

Requires credit repair organizations to provide consumers with the following written statement before any contract or agreement between the consumer and credit repair organization is executed. The statement must be separate from any written contract or other agreement, or any other written material provided to the consumer.

Consumer credit file rights under state and federal law

You have the right to dispute inaccurate information in your credit report by contacting the credit bureau directly. However, neither you nor any other credit repair company or credit repair organization has the right to have accurate, current, and verifiable information removed from your credit report. The credit bureau must remove accurate, negative information from your report only if it is more than seven years old. Bankruptcy information can be reported for 10 years.

You have the right to obtain a copy of your credit report from the credit bureau. You may be charged a reasonable fee. There is no fee, however, if you have been turned down for credit, employment, insurance, or a rental dwelling because of information in your credit report within the preceding 60 days. The credit bureau must provide someone to help you interpret the information in your credit file. You are entitled to receive a free copy of your credit report if you are unemployed and intend to apply for employment in the next 60 days, if you are a recipient of public welfare assistance, or if you have reason to believe there is inaccurate information in your credit report due to fraud.

You have the right to sue a credit repair organization that violates the Credit Repair Organizations Act. This law prohibits deceptive practices by credit repair organizations.

You have the right to cancel your contract with any credit repair organization for any reason within three business days from the date you signed it.

Credit bureaus are required to follow reasonable procedures to ensure that information they report is accurate. However, mistakes may occur.

You may, on your own, notify a credit bureau in writing that you dispute the accuracy of information in your credit file. The credit bureau must then reinvestigate and modify or remove inaccurate or incomplete information. The credit bureau may not charge a fee for this service. Any pertinent information and copies of all documents you have concerning any error should be given to the credit bureau.

If the credit bureau's reinvestigation does not resolve a dispute to your satisfaction, you may send a brief statement to the credit bureau, explaining why you think the record is inaccurate. The credit bureau must include a summary of your statement about disputed information with any report it issues about you.

The Federal Trade Commission regulates credit bureaus and credit repair organizations. For more information contact:

The Public Reference Branch
Federal Trade Commission
Washington, D.C. 20580
www.ftc.gov

Equal Credit Opportunity Act

Effective since 1975, this law was enacted to eliminate discrimination against women seeking to obtain credit. It was expanded to include the prohibition of denying credit based upon a person's race, color, place of national origin, religion, sex, age or marital status. It gives consumers the following rights:

- ❏ To be judged on an equal basis with all other credit applicants.
- ❏ To have joint accounts reported for both spouses separately after June 1977.
- ❏ To have income considered without regard to sex or marital status.
- ❏ To have regularly received child support and alimony payments counted as income, if requested.
- ❏ To not be asked questions about birth control or childbearing plans.
- ❏ To obtain credit cards in their own names if they are married women.

- To know the reasons they have been denied credit.

Fair Credit Billing Act

This act, in effect since 1975, gives consumers the following rights:

- To file a written complaint with the credit grantor within 60 days of the bill they question being mailed to them.
- To receive an acknowledgment from that credit grantor within 30 days of filing the complaint and a settlement within 90 days.
- To forestall collection of the account until the dispute is resolved.
- To prohibit that credit grantor from reporting negative information regarding the disputed amount to the credit reporting agencies until the dispute process is completed.

Appendix B

Where to Get Help

Debtors Anonymous is an effective support group for anyone with a debt or spending problem. It is based on the 12 steps of Alcoholics Anonymous, and there are no dues or fees. To get a meeting list or help in forming a chapter in your area, contact:

Debtors Anonymous
General Service Office
P.O. Box 920888
Needham, MA 02492-0009
(781)4 53-2743
(781) 453-2745 (fax)
www.debtorsanonymous.org
new@debtorsanonymous.org (e-mail)

Consumer Action assists consumers with marketplace problems. An education and advocacy organization specializing in credit, finance, and telecommunications issues, Consumer Action offers a multilingual consumer complaint hotline, free information on its surveys of banks and long-distance telephone companies, and consumer education materials in as many as eight languages. Write:

7171 Market St.
Suite 310
San Francisco, CA 94103
(415) 777-9365 (10 am to 2 pm PST) (consumer complaints)
(213) 624-8327
(415) 777-5267 (fax)
(415) 777-9456 (TTY)
info@consumer-action.org (e-mail)

National Consumer Law Center (NCLC) is an advocacy and research organization focusing on the needs of low-income consumers. It represents the interests of consumers in court, before administrative agencies, and before legislatures. Contact:

18 Tremont St.
Boston, MA 02108
(617) 523-8010
(617) 523-7398 (fax)
www.consumerlaw.org
consumerlaw@nclc.org (e-mail)

National Consumers League, founded in 1899, is America's pioneer consumer advocacy organization. The league is a nonprofit organization working to educate consumers in the areas of consumer fraud, food and drug safety, fair labor standards, child labor, health care, the environment, financial services, and telecommunications. The league develops and distributes consumer education materials and newsletters.

National Institute for Consumer Education (NICE) is a consumer education resource and professional development center for K-12 classroom teachers, business, government, and labor and community educators. NICE conducts training programs, develops teaching guides and resource lists, and manages a national clearinghouse of consumer educational materials, including videos, software programs, textbooks, and curriculum guides. Contact:

Eastern Michigan University
207 Rackham Building
Ypsilanti, MI 48197
(313) 487-2292
(313) 487-7153 (fax)
nice@online.emich.edu (e-mail)

The **Federal Trade Commission** monitors complaints related to consumer credit issues. Contact the Consumer Response Center:

6th St. & Pennsylvania Ave., NW
Room 240
Washington, D.C. 20580
(202) 362-2222
(202) 326-3502 (TDD/TTY)
www.consumer.gov

For public information from the Federal Trade Commission, write to:

6th St. and Pennsylvania Ave., NW
Room 130
Washington, D.C. 20580
(202) 326-2222
(202) 326-2050 (fax)

The **National Foundation for Consumer Credit** can help you establish a budget and repay creditors. For the office nearest you, call (800) 388-2777 or visit *www.nfcc.org.*

Appendix C

Addresses of Federal Agencies

The various federal consumer credit laws presented in this book are enforced by federal agencies. If you would like further information or have a particular credit problem that you would like answered, you can contact the appropriate agencies.

If your problem is with a retail department store, consumer finance company, all other creditors, and non-bank credit card issuers, credit bureaus, or debt collectors, contact:

The Division of Credit Practices Federal Trade Commission
Washington, D.C. 20580
www.ftc.gov

If you have a problem with a particular national bank, contact:

Office of the Comptroller of the Currency
Deputy Comptroller for Customer and Community Programs
Department of the Treasury, 6th F1.
L'Enfant Plaza Washington, D.C. 20219
www.occ.treas.gov

If you have a problem with a particular state member bank, contact:

Federal Reserve Board
Division of Consumer and Community Affairs
20th and C Streets, N.W.
Washington, D.C. 20551
www.bog.frb.fed.us

If you have a problem with a particular nonmember insured bank, or if you are uncertain of your bank's chartering (state or national), contact:

Federal Deposit Insurance Corporation Office of Consumer Compliance Programs
550 17th St., N.W.
Washington, D.C. 20429
www.fdic.gov

If you have a problem with a particular savings institution insured by the Federal Savings and Loan Insurance Corporation and a member of the Federal Home Loan Bank System, write to:

Federal Home Loan Bank Board Department of Consumer and Civil Rights Office of Examination and Supervision
Washington, D.C. 20522

If you have a problem with a federal credit union, contact:

National Credit Union Administration
Office of Consumer Affairs
1776 G St., N.W.
Washington, D.C. 20456
www.ncva.gov

Many of these federal agencies have regional offices. Check your local telephone book under "United States Government" to see if there is a regional office near you.

Appendix D
Federal Trade Commission Offices

The Federal Trade Commission is the agency responsible for enforcing the Consumer Protection Act. If a company has violated your rights under any of these laws, you can file a complaint with the nearest regional office. The FTC's Web site is *www.ftc.gov.*

Headquarters

Pennsylvania Ave. and Sixth St., NW
Washington, D.C. 20580

Regional offices

1718 Peachtree St., N.W.
Atlanta, GA 30367

10 Causeway St.
Boston, MA 02222

55 East Monroe St.
Chicago, IL 60603

8303 Elmbrook Dr.
Dallas, TX 75247

1405 Curtis St.
Denver, CO 80202

11000 Wilshire Blvd.
Los Angeles, CA 90024

26 Federal Plaza
New York, NY 10278

901 Market St.
San Francisco, CA 94103

915 Second Ave.
Seattle, WA 98174

Appendix E

Resources

Life After Debt (Career Press)
Not a rehash of old information, this book attacks the root causes of indebtedness and teaches consumers how to settle old accounts for pennies on the dollar. You'll learn how to stop collection agency harassment, billing errors and discrimination. Contains sample letters for reducing monthly payments, credit reporting disputes and negotiated settlements.

Life Without Debt (Career Press)
This companion to Life After Debt provides advanced strategies for surviving in this credit-oriented society. It reveals inside information about the credit system, from credit cards to home financing, student loans to cosigning for family members. It also contains special sections for dealing with the IRS, auto financing, bankruptcy and the psychology of debt and spending. Learn to save thousands of dollars on mortgages, auto loans and credit cards.

Credit Secrets: How to Erase Bad Credit (Paladin Press)
Contains a detailed description of the identification systems used by each of the major credit bureaus, along with dynamic strategies for

circumventing the system and starting over with a new credit file. Also describes a method of "losing" your bankruptcy files and deleting any reference to filing for Chapter 7 or Chapter 13.

How to Beat the Credit Bureaus: The Insider's Guide to Consumer Credit (Paladin Press)

Bob Hammond describes the deceptive web of information systems spun by the powerful corporate credit bureau syndicate and how it is used to victimize, humiliate and defile countless innocent consumers. More importantly, it will show you how to take legal action against an unfair system—and win. Includes documented successful lawsuits against major credit reporting agencies.

Index